The Whore

ISBN 978-1-955190-48-0
LCCN 2023932052

Designed, printed, and bound in the greater Seattle area

Design and typesetting by Joshua Rothes

Typeset in Linotype Sabon Next and Din Pro

MÁRCIA BARBIERI

The Whore

Translated from the Portuguese
by Adrian Minckley

an object by
SUBLUNARY EDITIONS
of Seattle, WA

THE WHORE

"[…] what existed then was a field of mirrors, Love appeared and disappeared in all of them, and we had to stay still and uncomprehending, for it was a child assassin and it walked the earth with its white shirts open, all its black and red shirts unbuttoned."

[*Animais carnívoros*, Herberto Hélder]

*[Prelude]. Yeah. That's what it was. I saw God's cracked vertebra. The sunset penetrating between his spinal discs. The hernia leapt out and pulsed in my vagina. It was the beginning of the Creator's decline. It was the coupling of God and Man. A strange bundle of happenings. The sun made my mouth bitter and opened fissures in my palate. Strange bodies lurked in the fissures—goblins, serpents—and decay hid in the folds. Decomposition begins when the pale monster is hung. Decomposition begins where the light is fickle. A botfly burrowed in my anal folds. A phallus in its right place. Before that tangled clarity, I spent night after night around the fire—I say night after night because at the time there weren't yet days to punctuate the darkness. The howl of the wolves warmed my shins, and I knew it was dawn when their canine uproar ended. At night, I listened to stories of men who didn't exist, ruthless animals that tore at their fellow creatures' flesh without shame or remorse. I heard tales of desperate women fighting over the love of a single man. And I already knew that my finger or those of another were

* I spied men sucking desperately (or was it hungrily¿) on primates' phalanges, they were in a circle. A bonfire heated the crossed-eyed night.

better suited than a cock could ever be. And I struggled to believe there was ever a time when women licked the open and erect wounds of men. I hardly spoke, my tongue was still imprisoned in the dense soil of my mouth. Sometimes I would hiccup, and maybe that sudden hiccup was a human remnant. I'd gather the sticks and break them with my teeth, the bonfire would crackle, and its red, yellow, violet, and blue flames grew. We had yet to hear of Moby Dick, had yet to chase the white whale. A fever perpetually consumed me, one hundred and four degrees. It was an aggressive son of a bitch, and the cold compresses never did anything but drench my headboard. That fever wouldn't let up; it was worse than scabies. My mother used to get scabies once a year, in summertime, whenever she went to the insane asylum. She always summered in the nuthouse. It was as if her biological clock knew what time she was supposed to go crazy, and she never made even the slightest effort to stop that clock from ticking. She'd come home itching all over—the mentally ill have poor personal hygiene, they like to roll around in each other's feces. She spent a third of her life in the company of lunatics, which strikes a lot of people as tragic, they feel bad for her, or think what a sad fate that must be, but she never seemed thrown by it. Quite the opposite, I always had the impression she felt less lonely and suicidal there than she did here. People devise morbid solutions to survive boredom, this bland staircase from nowhere to nothing, whereas lunatics are death-proof—they're surrounded by a strange protective energy. Her delusions coaxed her out of her lucidity, life seemed so clear to her it was almost blinding.

No one deserves to be victim to reality's whims. The few times I ever really heard her laugh she was locked up. I was never brave enough to ask her if she liked it on the inside. I was terrified of what the answer might be. Maybe she hadn't noticed that it's grim on this side, too; even if we paint it in lighter hues, our path is flanked on all sides by dead hands in free fall. The only thing she didn't like about the asylum was the electroshock therapy. She said they don't even let you go crazy in peace. They stuck those heaps of wires to her temples expecting a miracle, but nothing came of it except excruciating pain throughout her whole body, unbearable nausea, and temporary amnesia. But even then she managed to find an angle, because at the doctor's suggestion she started keeping a journal, and even enjoyed it for a few years, until she realized writing was a useless activity that didn't get her shit. Well, I guess it did get her a little something, because after filling a journal she would read it to the other lunatics, as long as they paid her in cigarettes. My mother became a chain-smoker and I acquired a strong aversion to tobacco. At least until I met Flamenca. I can tell you I had two mothers, one sane and unhappy, and the other, a reckless and contented lunatic. I don't know which one I liked less, I didn't identify with either of the two, and without a frame of reference to go by, I decided I was hatched by an unhappy incubator. When she had her outbursts, she'd scream: I can't stand reheated coffee, run quick, you little cunts, and bring me another one, from a different pot, this one's ruined, the devil took a piss in it. You're the one who let that abomination in, aren't you¿ You fucked him, didn't you, you little whore¿ Ask that deadbeat father of yours. What, he thinks just because Satan made you bread you have to eat it¿ What's that drunk son of a bitch thinking, that I'm just a goddamned incubator¿ Yes, my father. I never met him, thank God, because I doubt he's much different than my mother, but I know he thought that, and I thought it, and everyone else did too, which made me feel better because then I could imagine I hadn't inherited the genes for misery. What she wanted was to see me rip my hair out, a bald accomplice in her madness. Whenever she came back from the asylum, she'd spend hours recounting and laughing at her episodes. She would say that given the correct dosage of medications, insanity passed with the seasons, and she would shove the pills begrudgingly in her mouth until she inevitably went back to leaving full bottles lying around, probably because the crises were more taxing for others than they were for her. Why do I say that¿ Because she was self-centered, she thought her shit stank worse than everyone else's. But scabies (she kept scratching her arms bloody with her long, dirty nails) can sometimes take years to cure. And there was no point changing the sheets or boiling the towels. She was sure the bullshit in her head spread to her body through that terrible itch.† There was never a carnival happier than the lunatics' carnival, because their costumes were always loud. No sane person has

† My mother, the lunatic, would say she was never happier than during her time in the asylum. That's where she met her best friends and her most earnest lovers, and she might never have slept with a king were it not for madness. Madness is like that; it equalizes men through misfortune.

ever truly found happiness. I, on the other hand, opted for whispers and vagrancy. I would boil my clothes in the yard, my vision blurred by the soot from the wood stove, and throw everything in a large saucepan because I thought that by doing so I could free myself from the hassle of an ailment meant for dogs. But with time I came to understand that madness was not contagious, that it was only sad; the kind of sadness that makes your bones ache in winter. I don't like the cold, it makes me think about uncomplicated acts like dunking my head in ice water. And the heat makes me lazy and irrational. Don't you think there'd be less war if the world was hotter¿ Are there wars in tropical places¿ I don't think so! As far as I know there are only revolutions and they always fail. Just simmer off in the heat. Maybe we only die from epidemics, maybe our only cross to bear is the proliferation of insects. You don't need to push it, I already told you. It was a bloodstained femur, that's all I remember. I can't say if it was human or not, I'd done a lot of lines that night and, you know, when you're high, things take on unexpected proportions. I have a bad memory, life teaches us it's better to have a weak mind and a wilted mouth, just enough memories and words to keep the species going, and then here you come asking me to remember everything in perfect detail. Details are for pussies. Around these parts, living men have dead-men's mouths, and they stink like them, too. It's better left alone; birds that sing too loud end up in cages. We don't have time for things like that here, forget it! I don't remember the exact positions of the limbs or the angles the legs made with the moon. There were tibias and patellas of every size, but mostly stunted. A grotesque sight. I imagined that every type of displeasure was a flat angle, while anguish was obtuse, skinny, anorexic. The crooked geometry of those bright objects intrigued me. No, they weren't fetuses, they were a pile of dirty laundry, but in the dark, from afar, I don't know, anything is possible in this blind man's land. I also remember a guttural sound, like there was an animal being sacrificed, but I didn't smell any blood. An antelope¿ A goat¿ A horse¿ Don't be so stupid! How would I know, how could I have possibly made out horns in all that chaos¿! I assumed it had hooves because I heard some sort of galloping. Oh, cut me a break! There's no point! I don't know the difference between an antelope and a deer. Forget it, let's move on, we don't want to get off track, do we¿ Yes, enough. I've never been lucid, although sometimes the light gets in my eyes. I'm not sure if I'm cross-eyed or if the world is slanted.[‡] I've gutted more men than fish, because fish are rare and contested, and I don't regret it. I'm not complaining, don't get it twisted, it's a retelling, that's all. Just a ridiculous recounting of the facts that I saw or thought I saw or saw with a certain measure of difficulty. Better still, if you really want to know, I've had a few moments of weakness. I've never stopped to save a man, but I have felt bad for a few fish—usually the largest and most colorful ones, because they had more gumption, more stamina. For a

‡ I spent my entire adolescence blaming myself for the monsters I saw growing in the garden. I figured it was just my eyesight. Later, I discovered that some people saw lions, and others slayed large white mammoths, and so I convinced myself the deformed creatures were real.

while I even thought some of them might be able survive on land, develop shells, claws, lungs. I'm sure I was wrong, though I never followed up on any of their whereabouts, I just figured they were dead when I saw them bobbing in the surf. There's a lot more empty space in a man than there is in an invertebrate, I don't understand why they possess pulmonary function when gills could get you there no problem. Have you ever seen a man out of breath¿ What about a frog¿ What a waste it was to throw a backbone in to hold up the flaccid human soul. I've got more faith in the harpoon than I do in the net. The dawn blankets the night in viscera. A fistula erupts in my abdomen. I wish that philosopher motherfucker was here to talk about pain, about being, about metaphysics; his calculations left weak markings around the hole—hypotenuse leg square edge right angle—and he doesn't know how to get out anymore, isn't sure how to shirk this one. I don't understand a word, a single grunt that comes out of his stupid mouth, but I do get distracted by his babbling, and by the way his lips move. I'm amazed at what half a dozen books can do to an idiot's brain. His stupidity excites me, his words leaking out like slobber, a dead lizard lodged in his trachea. There's a pit lodged in my chest that takes up half my breast. And my breasts are synonymous with exile. I touch the nipples with the tips of my fingers, feel them harden. I caress the knots in the wood. I feel I'm an atom-piece of the soul of those inanimate objects. Tongue cocked, I take a taste of the wood that time enjoyed. I don't have much to say about the things I saw. What do you mean¿ You're saying I'm guilty because I was an eyewitness¿

You don't find that a little ridiculous¿ I'm an accomplice to a crime I didn't even know happened¿ And why would I have harbored a criminal¿ Am I worried¿ Why would I be¿ Worry is a loaded gun aimed at our temples and ready to blow. I don't lose sleep over it. People who don't sleep die faster. Oh, quit being pedantic, nothing like that happened, I wouldn't risk my life to save someone else's, I don't believe in heroes. I'm that shitty kind of woman that's already stopped believing in anything. I know the muscle-flesh was red and elastic, it was stretchy and slipped right off the bone. It was one of the strangest scenes I've ever witnessed—not that I'm a saint, far from it, but there was something scary about it all. The body was like a doll that had been torn apart by a child's hands. Right, left, I've always been an impatient and confused person, and strongly averse to cartography. Nowhere was my preferred refuge, and not even God could find me there. I admired the flying cockroaches that hid effortlessly in the gaps, then emerged from them like magic. I admired the kissing bugs that lived in the mouths of the hollow walls. I admired the rats that hid in the basement. I admired the men that masturbated the erect members of other men and waited anxiously for the liquid to explode. I was a fusion-egg of those four animal species, struggling to scale the cliff between two days. My soul lived in tatters; I tried to convince myself I wasn't just part of some humorless joke, but most of the time I found myself looking at my reflection in the bathroom mirror, and I discovered I was the undigested creation of a homicidal God. God birthed me then tried to hang me. I wasn't interested in the astronomy of daily life; the colors of the planets sickened me, made me vomit rotting stars. The majestic placements of the celestial bodies... The meteors opening craters and burying their dead. Nostalgia preserving fossils. The rotten egg of loneliness. I fed on that tragic embryo for a long time. I was conned into believing unaccompanied nudity would free me from ritual sacrifices and the goats that stalked me. Me and my fingernails, ruined, ingrown, spurting pus and sadness. No, I didn't run, what you witnessed wasn't an escape, it was... I don't know, I can't put a name to it... I didn't know what else to do, like I said, there wasn't anyone left in the village, almost everyone had died, and the ones who stayed ended up so far-flung they got lost.[§] All I wanted was to find them, I couldn't handle being trapped in that hole any longer. If I hadn't run, I'd be dead right now. Ten days of walking and I never found anything that stopped me, I rode a gentle horse for ten nights and the landscape never changed. The horse trotted on beneath a suicidal sun. I clip-clopped over the morning's bloody femur. I stemmed the blood that spurted from the femoral artery with one of the feet. I could have gotten down then, accepted the final spasms, and, after confirming the animal was dead, eaten it. I wouldn't have wasted a single limb, not one foot, not the nails, not the hooves, not the guts. I would have devoured its dying eyes. The eyes of all deceased are vast, obese, plump—that's why they have to be

§ There wasn't another option, it was necessary to defragment, molecule by molecule, a complete unfolding of the self. To become the multitude, to rape all the Russian nesting dolls.

removed, so death's secret isn't revealed, so no ghost sees and whispers in our ears on sleepless nights. Every departure covers my feet in cracks, as if some part of me also wanted to abandon this body, fragment itself. I'm not real, imaginary, or symbolic, I'm a given possibility and I exist in the negation of your cleft lips. I contort myself in the crevices in the roof of your mouth. My back splits open in cartographic stretchmarks. You can't eat the marrow without breaking the skin, stretching the muscles, cracking the bones, and all my bones are fractured. Each particle fills my body with despair. The shredded self. The splintered self. The flow of people, the ebb of me. One day, a long time ago, I had the ingenuity to think being abandoned wouldn't give me welts, and now I carry my vigils exposed on my naked and hairless flesh. My dawn breaks and I cough up hairballs. What would he think if he saw me so near these primates¿ Sometimes, I doubt he'd be able to tell me apart. I think he'd get us mixed up. He would explain rationalism and logic for hours, and I would nod my head, permissive, with my body pouring a sweat as dark and noxious as urine. The apes wandered around me, touched my hair, yanked at my earrings, laughing, howling at the state I was in. I hated seeing how similar I was to the monkeys, I hated how they looked at me, thinking themselves all superior with their long and agile members. What were they, after all¿ Horrendous, hairy monsters with large, dysfunctional brains. After the anger passed, I felt bad for them, and after I felt bad, I felt jealous of those animals' cries, of their exposed genitals, jealous of how easily they fucked and gave birth without answering to anyone. I birthed slender, shriveled beings, and everyone interrogated me as to the paternity of those delicate little men, as if I couldn't be capable of parthenogenesis. All the while, the fetus in the glass grew, even if it had yet to exist. But, according to the philosopher or lunatic, whichever you prefer, the past and the present coexist.¶ One is distension, and the other, contraction; I could feel his words while I caressed him, and he slid around and hardened in my hands. The past is, he whispered, and he lowered my underwear with the fingers I had just finished wetting with my spit. The past is, he continued, until his finger was muffled by my moaning. And time contracted and distended in my vulva and I thought, the heart is located in the cunt—systole and diastole, his cock inside me. You'll never be able to understand because your soul is masculine, ironclad. The only part of a man that isn't hooved is his dick. I'm three-toed like the rhinoceros. The one in the middle is colossal, ugly, heavy like a conscience and my conscience doesn't know how to live apart from the world. I still haven't grown out of the childish habit of hiding from indecisive creatures, seeking an empty corner, sitting down, turning my neck, looking sideways at my uterus, spitting on my unborn, licking my own thigh, tearing the hairs out with my teeth, tasting the salt on my skin, tilting my torso, crushing my diaphragm, splitting myself in two, reaching my mouth to my toenails and gnawing until I feel a trail of blood slide across my tongue.

¶ He still hadn't noticed that I was much more attached to instinct than to memory.

Rolling around on the banks of my strangeness. How can I see myself as separate from a man, how can I be indifferent to the cock that penetrates me, if a femoral vein runs along the periphery of my vagina, skirts the border of my asshole¿ Fucking makes me laugh and convulse and makes me remember that the place I came from is just as fucked as the place I am now. I wipe away the sperm that dribbles from my mouth and he kisses me before I'm done. He's methodical when he comes, one shot on the crotch and another on the throat. After sex, he makes improvised tweezers with his pointer finger and thumb and spends hours plucking his chest hairs while he denounces my slain nudity. Seeing him like that you'd never think he'd just finished scavenging around in the inconsistencies of my flesh. I'm a fallen being, foreign, and, touching my vagina I can't find any vestiges of relation with any known species—a flying fish sitting nude on the catastrophic edge of the bed, and I have no way of knowing what exists beneath my feet. I calculate the existence of a few venomous animals, but that isn't anything more than a possibility and the possibility hurts. Behind the door I recognize my likenesses; I'm nothing more than a cicada that lost its body, because what's left of me is the shell and not the filling. And the filling is a still life. We stayed that way, enveloped in our own carcass, quiet during the following three weeks, waiting for the door that was stuck shut to open. On the twentieth day it came unstuck, we placed our hand on it and it opened; we exited and didn't see each other again, or if we happened to reunite, weren't capable of recognizing each other. It was common to grow old in just a few days. It was common for couples to last just a few hours. He left and soon another man entered through my vagina, parted my lips and made himself at home. The gentle rain lasted two years, three days, and four nights. We discussed banal topics to distract ourselves from the fact we couldn't do anything but wait. He told me stories from his childhood. He told me he used to collect bedbugs in a jam jar, and that one day he came home to find his collection missing, his brother had chucked it. He stopped collecting things after that. I didn't think his story was interesting, but I did notice his eyes fill with tears when he mentioned brother. I decided it was better not to say anything, I didn't want to make things worse. If there was anything I found disgusting it was men crying and men who couldn't get it up, I didn't know what to do with either. I popped all the blackheads on his back, thinking that way time would go faster. It worked for a few hours. Then, I lowered down and cleaned out all ten of his toenails. But time didn't speed up. I started to almost enjoy his company. But time just kept inching forward. We counted the insects mating on the wall, laughed at the idea that insects could experience orgasms, might change positions to make it feel better. But time just stretched out farther. Other days, we would sit in silence, observing the snails that dragged themselves in across the muddy floor. He looked at me a little dirty because the trail the snails left behind looked an awful lot like the trails he left in my mouth. But time's slender fingers just kept growing. On Wednesday, we grabbed a clay pot and collected a few for dinner, they were tasty and nutritious, even though they looked disgusting, similar to okra but not green. But time was just a rock-hard cock jammed right up our asses. We heard earthquakes, and lightning slicing absurdity's edge. The thunder ruptured our dogs' eardrums. We had lots of dogs and had managed to construct a small hold to keep them in. The meat wasn't great but it kept us fed. I know that historically, people loved them and treated them like pets, but we didn't have the luxury of developing emotional ties to animals anymore. You know how it was, we were all suffering—we didn't even pamper members of our own species.** The storm got worse and the rainwater covered the roofs in gray moss. The flying insects got scared and stayed away for a few months. Our skin grew wrinkled, moist, and green. I looked more salamander than woman. Then, the storm, and the water surging, and the deluge pouring down in time's abyssal zone. I let the flood sweep me away. It was easy to let myself be taken by the current; my body knew to obey primitive commands. I dove under until I mixed with the liquid, until I let all my air out, until I couldn't see any more bubbles, until I couldn't hear my skin smacking against the water, until the sound didn't make sense anymore. Until nothing made sense anymore. Until all the notes merged in a single howl, a desperate grunt. The fractured oak. The dead fish bobbing above my smile. The other ear of silence. The dirty-yellow and pasty silence. The redundant echo of words. Circles and circles and drool trailing down

** At that time of extreme misery, cannibalism became a common practice for most of the population. We were no different than starving scorpions.

toward the breast and nothing said. A zoomzoomzooming of the ignorant. In every conversation, nothing more than the empty and emphatic functioning of language. The monotony corroded our taste buds. Talking was a chore because discussions were nothing more than a diagram; they were there, the questions and answers and each of their small variations—you made an x and then another x and then another x and then another—it was very simple, impossible to do wrong or get confused by. All of humanity's thoughts and thinkers were there. It was a game, a combinatorial analysis, and in my mind, what was the point¿ There was no way out of the ditch we'd dug ourselves. I walked around concerned with how to distance myself from silence if everything drew me towards it. The trachea pierced by the archangel's harpoon. The amygdala swollen with daydreams. Man dominated the word and the word hung him. Where else would it draw another breath¿ If it had two hands it would squeeze humanity's neck to hear the scream, hear the groan. God's gaping mouth, the spellbound tongue impregnated by the universe. I salivated dry, sandy globs, as if I had smoked pack upon pack of cigarettes, and recalled the finitude of my flesh, the dangerous curve of my hips, my holes sucking in men's attention, the stretch marks showing the way—all trails lead to the abyss and no one knew it—the ingrown hairs creating abscesses, the asymmetries making me human. My shell is my most fragile part. And my entire body is a shell. Imperfection brought me closer to the idiots and to the degenerates—I felt a constant attraction to the insane. I'm not ashamed to say it, I'd even venture to say that idiots are more apt at surrendering themselves to passion. I didn't think about the degeneration when their pubic hair rubbed against my clitoris, but this man was different, he wasn't a degenerate, wasn't insane. He Was, with the death of the verb. I met this fissured man, he was one and he was two, it was a binary game and I swear I wish I'd never laid eyes on him; he was impossible to live with because he was both the negative and positive pole within a finite piece of matter. I looked in his pupils and it was me inside, distorted, helical, hermaphroditic. Liquid and solid. He was alpha, and also omega. He would laugh and cry at the same time; with one hand he revived the desperate and with the other he drowned them. He provoked pity and hatred. He was a man and he had a vagina: BEAUTIFUL, MASSIVE, the most perfect I've ever seen. A split, a tear, a rift, a pseudo-hole. His generous scrotal sac orbited his taut thigh. He had a rosy hollow between his legs. A shredded octopus on his pelvis. A couple labia hung almost to his knee, which was what made him so much like me... Maybe that's why he found me so convenient... because I too was bothered by that flesh that fell so far it almost skimmed the surface of anguish. Maybe that's why I saw myself through him. I felt like a grafted plant, a hybrid without fixed roots. His disjointed and arid breasts hung over his chest cavity, those foul teats no child would ever feed from. It's a privilege to meet your double. Few get the chance. Most starve to death without ever meeting theirs. It was a frameless mirror that appeared in front of me. Some called it a sign of good luck. People say whatever pops into their heads. The mad have no filter, they don't know when to shut up. I like the silent, pale creatures hanging on cold mornings with scars on their faces. Fish meet death through their mouths, men are used to creating sores, wounds spread like wildfire across their mouths, they bite the hook but don't swallow, just leave it caught there till it drags fatigued/filleted through the esophagus. Scission, I read that word in story once and I never forgot it. It's a sad word, with disgrace at its core. I had an affinity for tiny outcasts, that's why I fed the beetles, the cockroaches and scarabs I found in the darkness-sewer-booby-trap that was his lips. I didn't kill lice or ticks; I buried them alive instead. Split, that's how I was from the very beginning, when I saw him through the mirror back there; at first, he was nothing more than a black dot, small and diffuse, a speck. I was bipartite when drool settled on my chin, when I still didn't have any sense that things divided themselves into eras, and my spinal column still ended in a tail. Sometimes my tail still hurts, as if my coccyx had no end, an appendage out in the world. I know no one needs to hear this small talk. I glue my ear to the wall. I like the whispers, the sound of the insects devouring the wood. I hold my breath to hear them better. A mosquito sleeps on my face—I stir—it goes in my nose and out my mouth. I move my attention across to the other side. I'm roused by the sound. A knife being sharpened on a rock. The steel softening the rock's dream, the ground curdling, life decanting, cells populating rivers, the first autotrophic beings emerge. Glass crushed by a lunatic's tactless hand. Lunatics hate other lunatics. Identification. Asylums were abolished, there were too many crazies to hold.

Now the world is our asylum, no gates, no strait jackets. We walk around naked and no one would dream of punishing us for it. I sleep and I dream of the universe's pollution contaminating the wounds in my uterus. I suck his fingers, one by one, and his hands. It was a single finger (I think of the solitude of masturbation), and the fingerprints were numerous. Refractory men. I glance at my face. My profile carries fileted sadness. An ant distracts me. It reaches its destination and I watch as it joins the others in devouring a dead rat. I'm not brave enough to look at myself for any prolonged period. I am condemned by everything I'm not. After a long time searching I find the white whale; it's floundering, beached[††]. The acne abandoned my skin. My teeth are losing their lacquer, yellowing, my canines have gone dull. My arch less prominent. No signs of youth anymore. What rotted away was the best of me. My punctured orbit still holds memories. A plantar wart erupts on my left foot. It stares at me and I stare back. I poke it with the tip of a knife until it bleeds. I give the area a once-over. Sometimes it feels like my habitat is separate from myself, foreign, not attached to my limbs, a feathered tail that isn't mine. I try not to waste time thinking about such pointless things, I breathe, and get distracted by something else. A bird sings and all I can think is what kind of trap might hold it. The outside extends so much farther than the body does, and yet still we refuse to explore it. Here, the orange frame decouples

†† I've searched for the white whale for years, I was there at its birth. I saw its body inflating and thrashing-swallowing the maternal body. I understood that copulation was the mirror-simulacrum of death.

from the mirror. I try to remove it, but I can't, my hands tremble. I hear the knife sharpener dragging his cart. His beard touches the ground. One of the few survivors. Before the war, he killed his wife with one of his knives because he found out she wasn't just one man's woman. That her body demanded multiple pleasures, that she liked the feel of other men's tongues between her legs. What's wrong with that? Let he who casts the first stone be the one who has never imagined getting licked by a tongue of every thickness. Every day he goes by at the same time *el knife for el silver coin*. No one carries around coins anymore. He knows it but pretends he doesn't. Not knowing is less painful. Mounds of salt disappear slowly. Who needs truth? I repeat: *el illusion for una silver coin*. I blow my nose, my nostrils are as wide as a fat woman's hips. The leftover cocaine puffs out between my face and the frame. The white whale is still floundering, beached. I try to remove the sand with my paddles, but they're fragile—I can't do anything but watch in admiration as the white monster gets devoured by the sand. My septum seems to dislocate from my skull. Mandibles quivering, my teeth careen out my mouth. My square face splinters. Anima animus, my sex, a concave spherical mirror, inverted images. I do a bunch, respecting the limit of the mirror's edge. They weren't wrong, a mirror is a mythical object, it connects two, three, four worlds, five dimensions. I dab a little on the tip of my tongue to see if it's the good stuff. I miss the days when you could find powder on any old corner, when every street kid knew a guy. I also sold drugs for a while, not a lot, a few grams a day—just enough to cover my own habit. I never made any money from it and I never killed any addicts. Doing lines is the beginning of perdition. It smells white, almost blind. I look facing-forward, then in profile, squinting, my face dilates, contracts in some sort of pompoir. The mouth expelling the sleeping embryo. The cord falling from the epicenter. Outside, the same hole. The crabs awaiting the rain before rising to the surface. The ground taking up space. A vine playing the role of a bush. The bones piling up in one corner. Giant, worthless mammoths. The smell of carrion is sickening. If the sun was any stronger I wouldn't be able to hold my vomit in. The fat, dying flies bobbing in the heavy air. The schizophrenic birth of the sun. My knees hurt. Three hours squatting without moving, hips cracking from the weight of my shoulders. My kneecap dislocates from my femur, it's like it has a mind of its own, I try to put it back in place, but I'm not strong enough. My hands tremble and sweat. I look out through the orifice in the front wall. I can't take squatting anymore to make myself fit. I request clemency. An entire life spent squatting to avoid the sunset. Radii and diameters measuring absence. I make an imaginary line from bust to tibia. Distance is more fluid than we could ever understand. My body suffers the erosion of the winds, a plane becoming a depression.[‡‡] The living imitate the rituals of the dead. A dagger slices the night's opaque heat. Scratches the world in half. A well-carved wood cutting. The night arrives despite me. The dawn arrives despite God. Graffiti on the white walls that

‡‡ The plane is the primary architect of the cave.

separate the Town from the rest of humanity. An odor rises from the defense trenches and the moats. Humans reek of corroded iron. Fish spawning. A mother after birth. Wet dog. Yesterday, the fisherman spent four hours watching the water beat against the rocks. He doesn't expect to see fish anymore, he's lost interest in the things the ocean swallows. The taste of the seeds that wiped out the crops is still floating on my saliva. I couldn't resist, I was supposed to save them, but I was so hungry it was staggering. When I chewed the seeds, it was like I was swallowing-strangling millions and millions of fetuses, of men, of women, of old people and children. My hunger wiped out an entire village. There's still something in my mouth that's rancid, nostalgic. I examine the world and bite my tongue. My spit is thick, caustic, tastes like aged hatred. Ruination made me multiply, vast flesh, strong roots spread out among the tombs of strangers. My limbs are foreign and distant from my fingers. I don't feel bad for men who mourn their luck. Rummaging around among ancestors and embryonic characters, I'm able to place men and rats in the same subgroup. Weakness makes me nauseous. I don't give advice to suicidal people. But I still pray for them. I plant rue leaves behind my ear. None of them seem interested in growing. I go quiet. The staggering silence of the milk spilling and spreading its thick cream. Disguising the ember. Greasing up the night. Blanching the view perforating the mucous undoing us churning the intestines blowing in your shitty anus. Anal douches can't solve the problem anymore, it's your soul that's rank. I tried to warn you, but you never listened, only pretended,

pretended to hear while you ruminated on your ideas, all those ideas you had to formulate to be called a philosopher. And for what?—I ask. They didn't offer you anything, weren't your soul's salvation. Your bone marrow squirts out heartaches and you can't handle it. You don't even know the difference between a scratch and a gaping wound. A gill severed the night and you keep on breathing, unaware, a woodlouse that ends in itself. You forgot your tongue between my legs and now you're mute. Strangled by silence. Muteness corrupts worse than the crowd. I knew that one day I'd catch you by surprise, I knew you'd come crawling back holding your severed tail in your hands. Your horrible attitude shocks me. Your bulging belly fights for space between the serpents. I feel around, searching for the fetuses you consumed. I don't find anything, I'm in awe of your ability to hide the obvious. Your bulging belly makes me remember your insect form. Why keep making up lies if I already know everything? Kids' words and crabs confuse my epidermis. And the executioner expounds for hours and hours on humanism while you lick my asshole like a desperate dog. You wanted to speak, took our transgressions against the great despots as your own. I don't understand, at this point you should already know there's no going back. You're locked in here with me too, take a whiff of the sewage in this hole, there's no escape. I believed, a few times I believed in you, thought you were a little stronger. I thought that aside from a cock, you had guts, too. Poor me, you're just a castrated scholar. You know everything went wrong. You're not in control anymore—I doubt you ever were. I never liked sleeping with philosophers. Between one fuck and another, a flawed metaphysics. Ontology. Escape routes, bifurcations. He looks to the sky and tallies the moon's stretch marks. He searches for the universe's clit while mine is here throbbing, crying out for a tongue to soothe it. He asks forgiveness for the pleasure he didn't give me. He says my bones weren't stable, that my pelvis wouldn't have been able to handle the kind of pleasure he knows how to give. He could lay waste to my muscles with a single breath. He says I'm weak, and he, verbose. He rambles on about atoms and constellations, can list the name of every tributary. I like you, you know. You know I'm not good at the mechanics, I like fucking you, so I like you, I don't need to keep saying it like some kind of sacred ritual. Sometimes, I know I trip you up, I make your life harder, my brain is a centipede and each defiant foot takes off in a different direction and my whole head falls apart in the process. Imagine a hundred feet destroying minuscule matter. Can you picture it? That's how I feel. I like your pussy, the exposed labia minora-majora hanging off your vulva, it's my bell of inquietude. I want you to understand: the things that have been happening aren't my fault, I wasn't prepared, I'm a man of the mind and pounding rebar is too corporeal, it's within the realm of matter and matter is unstable. Our bodies are deceptive, my dear, they distract us from the true climax—climax isn't the ejaculate from my cock that splatters across your chest. When you care about love you also have to care about the tragicomic. I can't penetrate you the way I used to, I've been thinking, what matters isn't profundity, the true philosopher understands the importance of the things that hang low, on the sides, it's the surface that's important, that's why you have a false penis on top, slotted away above the vagina, because the vagina is the organ of depth, of trickery, it's the organ that deceives men. You and your little treatise can go fuck yourselves. How are you planning on paying? I'm not getting sucked into this pointless game. I'm a beast and that's how I like it, don't try to make me any less of an animal. Dogs eat their own shit, and that's their thing, the instinct of the imprisoned dog that wants to keep its cage clean. My skin reeks of naïf sexe. There's no need to explain stolen pleasures to a bitch. Don't come at me with minced words, nicely measured and sanitized, I like words that roll around in shit. Your non-being won't convince me you're frail. I was also born on the outside, cultivated outside the uterus, in this iteration of a white divide made for the unfit, and even still I don't shy away from the pleasure of a good fuck. That philosopher son of a bitch's tongue can't make me come. Quite the opposite, the density of it makes me sad, pushes me outside the world, casts me as a public good. My vagina, a black hole, anti-matter, ancestral nothingness. It's better to never be born than to live in the howl. Hours and hours calculating latitudes and longitudes, names of constellations, stars in the shape of earthly animals—hydra dog bear scorpion—an astronomy of abysses. How to scrutinize my pussy without sublimating-disappearing? I masturbate, play with my clit, and in the white clearing I see God's swollen pussy, beautiful, shining out between two legs. If the epiphanies of men—those dim, minuscule lanterns—

are intolerable and hold the power to rupture their blood vessels, break their tibias, crack their iliac crests, make their synapses go haywire, imagine what would happen if God dabbled in them too... Not a single tectonic plate would manage to right itself before shattering to pieces, every mirror would become sand and sand would reflect asymmetrical profiles, no continent would survive, the imaginary lines would implode, woman would carry her fallopian tubes in the palm of her hand to save the act of creation and man would be nothing more than a negligible speck amidst God's thoughts. Don't look at me from the false corners of your eyes—a rock rises in front of you—you were the one that chose this liquid state, this trip around the universe's duodenum; I'm solid, raw material, simplification. Your non-form does nothing for me. Being slippery isn't a quality, it's an escape, it's cowardice. I can't observe the poverty of scaly fish, but I do like weak men, because it's like I own their limbs and could amputate them whenever I wanted. It's like I'm squeezing their balls between my fingers. I DON'T WANT TO. I'd rather spend my time removing my vertebrae with pliers so I can fit into this cubbyhole called the world than subject myself, bury myself in your resurrected lizard skin. I can't pay you to contemplate me. The ocean exists and doesn't need you—face that wisely. Pleas are the same as dead dogs' purple tongues. I think of the power of crocodile jaws while I squat over your fear. Forgive me if here your books can only be used to light fires and your theories are nothing more than the hallucinations of an ailing mind. Your schizophrenia doesn't exonerate you of your faults, the shit you hide beneath your nails—your world was born of a desperate fungal infection. Why do the insane presume their own innocence? Why do they think they have permission to commit their premeditated and heinous crimes? Your lunatic voyage to whisper in my ear is boring. I extend my arm so you can inject your vaccinations while I lose myself in a convulsive hysteria. Your pocket change can't be counted. Your sacrifice is a meteor shower on dry nights. Your nasal tubes don't move me. I'm not moved by this leakage of yours, this matter overflowing the folds of your obese body, this solitary and morbid fat. You get distracted counting the nodules in your flesh, thinking cysts only grow on well-endowed, superior spirits. I make a cut on my thigh and stick your fingers in—I want you to see that reality is dirty, obscene. I want you to dig around in my limb's rot. You balk, suggest I insert a catheter to keep the wound open and to let some of the dirty blood out, but you end up liking the blood smell and lick your middle finger slyly. The fissures of collapse are already present in love's embryo-birth. The fistula, the fissure, the finale, beginning's other end. A ball ready to be rolled. Entire peoples were exterminated and for better or worse we survived. We carefully remove the shrapnel and you sit there contemplating the ruins so you can describe them. As if we needed your minute descriptions to understand tragedy. You say the world will begin again by narrating the destruction. The innocent God of destruction. Chaos arrived a long time ago and you're the only one who isn't hip to it. After the rain comes the sun, and after the sun, the giant ants rise from the earth ready to die. We roll over in our sleep and scare ourselves. We rotate our masks, but the grimace remains. The farce remains, the face-deforming clay. The outline laughs at the finished work's pretention. As children, we played our evil off as innocence. Now they want answers, but only lunatics and artists delineate hypotheses. Art is a safe way of preserving life, making it less ridiculous, less miserable, even comical. Life would be unbearable if it couldn't be narrated. Dribbled between one comma and another. A bonfire tells a story and continues. The fire goes out and continues. He who tells stories unravels in daydreams. Once upon a time. In the beginning, the Almighty created heaven and earth. The earth was void and empty. The worms had yet to corrupt God's porous flesh. Now, post-apocalypse, the earth returns to the vacuum, to dullness. I look through the slot in the rotten wooden window, mountains of salt getting lost slowly. I nurture myself on that loss, that natural erosion.[§§] From afar the whiteness looks beautiful, we get closer and the wind blows salty in our mouths, dries-cracks the skin. My herpes broke out six times this year. Weak immune system, they say. I've always been pursued by morphetic beings. My muscles ache, but they just won't quit. I can't stop running. They're still after me, getting closer and closer, I can almost feel their hairs brushing my calves. A rusty screw traverses the afternoon. Existence grows straighter, fitting inside itself. It loses meaning. No, I don't mind, I'll start over so you can

§§ when I was a child I admired erosion's omnipotence, its power to change the shape of large things. Still today it scares me.

understand me better. That's exactly what you heard. It wasn't a daydream. It wasn't a schizophrenic outburst. It was there, I saw it. A big strong man was dragging something, it must have been a body or some remains (of an animal?). He limped, had a hard time walking. His back was huge. He wasn't fat, that's not what I said, I said he had broad shoulders, he was robust. Maybe he seemed shorter because he was limping. It was impossible to tell if the blood was from his bad leg or from the body he was having a hard time dragging. Alright, I'm not sure, maybe it wasn't a body, it could have been a sack of rice or something else entirely. But why would someone carry a sack of rice around in the shadows in the middle of the night? The thing is that it was snowing, the night was so white it was like the whole earth was covered in cocaine (although now that the war is over I can hardly ever find the stuff), and it was good—I mean the feeling was good, not the lack of cocaine. I kept following the sack man out of the corner of my eye. He turned for a moment and I got scared, I thought he was staring at me, but that was impossible, because there's no way he could see me. I don't know where I got that idea from. I broke out in a cold sweat. Have you ever experienced that? I never had before. The sweat was running down my face, I used the back of my hand to wipe it away, but it soon began flowing again and heavier and heavier until I gave up wiping it. I took a deep breath; the tip of my nose was frozen and my nostrils were red and swollen. I remembered Gogol's "The Nose", because it seemed that at any moment my nose would fall off my face and take up a life of its own, which kept me busy for a while, as absurd as it might sound. Of course, consciously, I knew my nose couldn't escape, and that it would stay right where it was, static on my face for years. I know, I know, it doesn't usually snow here, but that night... One thing I am sure of is I don't know exactly how I managed to fall asleep or what I dreamed about, I felt like I got whacked in the neck and when I finally woke up, it was Fall, the snow had already melted and the man and the carcass were gone. I probably slept for a couple hours, two and a half at most. I know it's unbelievable, but that's what happened. Go ahead, write it down. Don't get nervous, at your age, and in your line of work, I would have already gotten used to strange things—who knows, I might even have started believing in miracles. (I'll move on) I took up tarot when I was young to distract myself, pretending to guess what was already so obvious. Do you want me to read your cards? Life starts to regain its meaning, I lay the white towel on the table, I place the cards—the hanged man, he rises from the dead strangled in the obscene openings of the larynx and the epiglottis. Swallowed dry. The throat is a rough sketch of a pussy. And my pussy has bunions. Put your hand here, you can feel them. Every day they ram a hard cock up our asses. And they take it out right before we come. I count my interrupted intercourse in the cracking of the days. The hangover tears-bursts the mornings. Annunciation. Again they shout, again the echo replies, Annunciation. I like the wetlands and the intermittent rivers that are sometimes deserts, promise, the lingering expectation of rain, lizard dwellings, children walking in the depths. We grow and float on the surface, aerated matter, the beetle's whirring, a boil on God's perfection. Crab eyes scare me, they're movable, human eyes, and accusational. Not that I'm prone to guilt. That guilty feeling that drives people to charity was not a trait I inherited. I have the instinctive hunger of an animal. I advocate for monsters. I perform vivisections on rabid dogs, I like to watch their hearts pumping. I don't believe in first-time offenders. There's no one to run to, each judges their own flesh. Horses can only hear the sound of their own hooves—to each the salvation of their own skin. Mine is singular, a fly roost. A larval respite. What were you imagining? Someone asking permission and clearing away your wreckage? Someone licking your burial shroud? Watching your every move? Here, eyes are two hollow pits in your face. Here all the dead are buried nude. Their muscles dislocate from their bones, torn like tattered elastic. Their clothing is given to the youth and their jewels stolen by our most promising minds. You don't take them with you. Let's make that real clear. You don't deceive the devil. Walk without moving your feet out the mud. You won't sink, trust me, your soul carries the weight of those who are unconscious. Scream all you want, sound doesn't travel in a vacuum. The only thing you can do is count your wounds, lick the sperm leaking from your abdomen, feed off yourself. The pustules still spread rapidly across your body—you'll soon give birth. You might not agree with me now, but afterwards, you'll lick my pussy to reward me for being right. I wake up and keep the windows closed. Silverfish sleep between the slats. Those tiny creatures have always intrigued me. They've been like that for thirty years, like an unseeing eye on a suicidal man's face.¶¶ Your wounds keep spreading the cavity throughout your body, the hollowness of your soul. I can't do anything for you, the bandages are useless. The soot from inanimate objects sticks during orbit. The atoms divide, but never dissipate—immortality is in the proton, neutron, nanomaterial of the rock. The moss, a living being, animate, green, the flower's preamble, scrutinizes but doesn't tear the rock's skin. If you could cleave it, you'd see there's nothing there but a viscous and lonely cavity. If you stuck your tongue in the gap you'd know there's no way to masturbate it. No one will help, things are different now. You're still naive, seeking responses in an ancient world that came apart easy like poorly knit fabric. Even though our population is negligible, we'll still have to endure epidemics and there's no hope for a vaccine, our hands are tied. We don't have any doctors to dole out miracle injections. Antibiotics are no longer available. We could die of tetanus at any time. We'd have to return our hands to the sky and clamor for some deity, any one will do, a heaven, a sun, a tree, a dismembered body. Do you want me to call my mother over? She's been over there, seated in that chair since the day she birthed me. I can ask my mom to bless you, she's a healer, all she has to do is drink some tea and go into a trance, commune with the sacred; here insanity is a privilege. In another time, the neighbors would have locked their doors, called the police,

¶¶ A Celtic legend says that suicides arrive in hell blind, God plucks out their eyes so when they look to the sky, they can't see the wonders of paradise.

and sent her straight to the asylum, but now, the few neighbors we have left can't even imagine what an asylum might be. My mother has regained her prestige and sometimes I even forget how much I used to hate her, how much I used to cry during her schizophrenic outbursts. I know it's not much to a philosopher, but for those who believe strongly in the Self, I don't find it too unreasonable to believe in prayers and palm fronds. How many tomes did you have to read to not believe in anything? People who are atheists for political reasons are ridiculous, just because they read a well-written text. You're a test-tube skeptic, it's not genuine. It wasn't life that made you a non-believer, it was your footnote conversations, the scribbles at the end of the page. Which of your philosophers saved you from ruin or gonorrhea? Syphilis feasted on your brain and you didn't even notice—couldn't tell how big the hole was. Even sick you were snobbish, kept speaking in incomprehensible dialects, didn't want to mix with the large and ignorant masses. You used to say that woman held the semen of misfortune, that's why you were chaste for years. And you were right, the pussy is a putrid hole. We carry the germ of humanity in our tubes—nothing that multiplies can be innocent. You had infected milk in your cock, too, but you pretended not to see it, your eyes were addicted to contemplating distant objects. The outside was the primary subject of your misguided theses. But did you take a look at your dick? It was completely raw, shot out noxious green pus, and what did those higher minds do for you? None of them wanted to pierce you for fear they'd get contaminated. You were scared, too, and asked me to rub your back. A coddled beast. I don't take orders, I invent them. I did only what gave me pleasure and touching you when your flesh was penumbral gave me none. I refused; your skin was scaly and dry, like a fish plucked from its natural habitat. I thought of the axolotls I'd never met, and their morbid similarity to humans. I thought of the dismay of encountering gravel so mixed in the waters, of the sun that careens down every afternoon. It took you a long time to learn that verbs are distant from action is is is and that stutter wasn't mine. Verbs are entombed in grammar. The body houses the strong and the soul is for people with time to spare. The majority of men only discover they're alive once they get skinned, after they look in the mirror and contemplate their bruises—before that they look more like amoebas. Your glans still carries the scars of other uteruses, other tongues, other tragedies. I don't watch your performances anymore. You've never really faced sadness, you asked me to make an infusion with some kind of hallucinogenic plant (the mandrakes that grew beside the cemetery of the unborn), and afterwards, you laid alone in the dark and jerked off five times as if pleasure could make the pain worth it. Pleasure and pain are fruit of the same sputum. And you seemed to want to tease out the fruit. You sliced at the flesh until you arrived at the pit's hollow soul. I was already used to teasing it out, I already knew the pit was noisy. I liked to feel it beating around in my teeth's solitude. I also knew doing all that work was pointless, but I didn't see any reason to say anything. No one told me, some things we have to see for ourselves. It's not worth it, you won't be happy draining all the sperm from your scrotal sac, milking it into your hands won't alleviate your boredom. The shower won't get you clean, your muscle-flesh is cracked, a poorly built wall, fragile in its most base structures. I caress your embryonic crevices with the back of my tongue, I can't tell where you lost yourself—you originated this way, a bifid man. Son of a detached placenta, out of place. You don't need to explain it to me, coddle me with your empty discourse, you don't have an audience anymore, all your disciples are dead, off wandering through the matte white nothingness. You aren't worth a penny—I could stab you and I wouldn't feel bad. Stab you like a puppet just before the curtain falls. I could cut all your strings and watch you collapse. I prefer to touch myself while I drag on a Cuban cigar, it levels me out. People should smoke and fuck more. Sometimes I dream about how Cuban men fuck, do you think it smells the way the cigars do? I think about the obscenity of musicians' finger work. Hours and hours strumming the same note. An incessant croaking makes my ear prick up. Outside there's a river of frogs mating, filling the night's scowl, darkness is boil-covered flesh. I watch the amphibians mating again, they're adaptable beings, that's why they can multiply without shame. I run my hand along the insides of my thighs, I can tell they're starting to get flaccid, but the tradeoff is that my pubic hair is still black, I can't find a single gray one, and I still ooze liquid—as long as it's moist I'm still living. I cry for the cactus that will one day be born from my vulva, when it becomes dry land, granular. I peer through the hole where the key should fit. I see solitary men tallying the intestinal folds.

They count to ten and make a knot then count again until every mathematical possibility has been spent. Loneliness—geometric progression. The vastness is sad to behold from afar—a tooth's decay-hole. Dead asphalt dog. ?How many suffering dogs have you kicked at your front door? I move the earth around and see a fetus being devoured by leafcutter ants, I squat down thinking I'll save it, then notice it's just a severed ear. Our desperation begins in the ear. It spreads our cries across the threshold. The poet invented the laugh to redeem him of his suicides. Ignore the fresh corpses he carries on his back. The sun departs every day behind him. How many sunsets can his vertebrae support? Behind me is always yesterday. I died three hundred times and three hundred times I rose. They broke all my wooden legs. Scraped my skin, slurped up all my marrow. Ripped out my molars with tweezers. I recompose myself like a white house gecko. A yellow lizard before creation. A flawed fossil of my ancestors. *God is only an abstraction*, a Greek chorus whispered in my good ear. Few things remained intact after the birth, after the embryo grew, writhed, spat on the uterus. A massacre of children is tragicomic. War is a less perverse method of birth control, they say. They kill potential mothers and fathers. You can't make a litter if you don't fuck. Siblings had their way with each other and invented incest. Siblings cut off other siblings' heads and invented homicide. They busted teeth out and invented the smile. In primitive societies war is less necessary. They practice infanticide. Children are tossed from their mother's embrace or forgotten without food. Everything around here is going back to mythic times too. We lost it all. The population dropped almost to zero. The few that remained decided to spread out, with fewer people per square kilometer it would be easier to survive, and the food would last longer before running out. You have to be careful because the ones that stayed defend their territories tooth and nail. Even so, I decided to stay with what was left of my family—my mother—and try to rebuild a life. We don't have comfortable houses, technology, or food anymore. We've reverted to hunter-gatherers. And even so what we catch ain't much. Domesticating animals is hard, they're reserved, they don't trust that their owners are innocent, and most of them escape before getting caught because they intuit their end is near. The bombs' chemical compounds made the earth infertile. All the knowledge we had was reduced to ash and the medical advances, well, they died along with the last of the doctors. We only have one doctor now, Muñozito, that's what everyone calls him, he survived, but wouldn't you know, he came from a wealthy family and they'd bought him his diploma, his parents always wanted him to be a doctor but he'd never been interested in medicine. He had everything he wanted, didn't need to work and spent all day reading erotica and fucking whatever woman fell for his sweet talk. He was only a doctor on paper. Post-catastrophe, he saw an opportunity to make a name for himself and now his goal is to be the first doctor of the new age. Doctor Muñoz—that's what he wants to be called now—he's really working for it, he travels the darkness with a helper, a real-life Sancho Panza, snagging animals and dead men to dissect. The doctor says the first step is to create a new nomenclature, which is why he's analyzing dead bodies, to discover and touch every muscle, every bone, every digit. I don't really trust his work, but we don't have much of a choice, he's one of the only people who knows even a little about anatomy, after him there's the dentist, the butcher, the cook, and whatever midwives were left over. I'm also among the few survivors and for some inexplicable reason I've been alive for over a hundred years, even if I don't look a day over forty. Like I said before, my mother regained the prestige of an ancestral age. In modern times, no one had any respect for curandeiras or xamãs. On top of the mud wall there's two meters of bottles with herbs in them, plants and roots of every color and size. My mother managed to salvage a mandrake root from the ruins; thanks to her we can now take advantage of its hallucinogenic powers and honestly, how did anyone survive back then without getting high¿ We needed distractions from suffering. I liked to watch the mandrake growing inside the pot, its limbs spreading out in the transparent waters, its rhizomes confusing everything, it looked like an amniotic sac—anything could have been growing in there, a horrible monster, an insane person, or an innocent child. But I never believed in innocence, nothing good could be born so openly, so unconcerned with showing how its organs form. It was like watching a fetus grow in a jar. Mom liked to tell the story of a quiet boy, a fat, pasty, mute boy, no one knew for sure where he came from but they all knew something was off and some say they saw how he emerged. They said he was a mandrake, but that he grew and grew so much he ended up as flesh incarnate with a sprouted soul. I'm not sure I believed the story, but she'd pick me up off the floor and I liked that, I liked floating while people told me things. Sometimes when I stop to think, it makes sense to me, after all, I've met enough soulless men along the way, why get hung up on a plant made flesh¿ You should know, I'm sure you do—where are you from¿ Are you really from this village¿ Because if you are, you should already know that before the war we went to clinics for everything, expensive ones for the rich or pigsties for the poor. But now we've gone back to mysticism, and these days my mother is one of the most important women in town. She's the midwife and doctor, she drives out our demons. Makes medicines out of weeds. You might call her one, but she's not a witch. She knows about herbs is all. She knows that the illness carries the seed of its cure. If it weren't for her intuition we'd already be dead like the others. The people who survived the war weren't the most cultured, hence the difficulty in regaining all the science we lost. But we knew one important thing: that things are born, grow, and die. Our old civilization went into decline and snuffed itself out, and we had to start over from scratch. But I noticed quick enough that not much had changed for the whores. Our work was the same, except that now we didn't have any protection against sexually transmitted diseases. But even when we did, most of us had preferred not to use it. Even without protection, I've spent a long time getting fucked with no problem. Just the recurring herpes, but I already had that on my mouth before the extermination. I lost hearing in one of my ears after the war. We all have a price to pay and I didn't consider mine very high, but being deaf is a big inconvenience. The bullet traveled for kilometers and then it went quiet, laying await in ambush. It moved on the sly, passing through my skull until it got lost in my brain's meandering middle. I was lucky to survive, put your finger here, you can still feel where it went. I get crazy headaches, but I have something no one else in the village does, though if anyone knew what I'm hiding I'd be dead. In the golden age of the whorehouse—before the war that ruined everything—I had a regular who was a doctor, and he gave me oil of vitriol: distilled sulfuric acid and alcohol, better known as ether. He taught me to like ether even more than I liked cocaine or Cuban cigars, he'd bring vials of the stuff and all the whores together would do what he called the ether revelry. I managed to save a few vials. I use it religiously to manage my pain, and sometimes for emergencies, too. My mother has done amputations and cesareans and I've suggested she use the ether, although of course the patient can't know. Even now I hear dead fingers on the porous wood, I'm still deciphering Morse code. I know no one uses it anymore. It's not worth a shit, but who cares what futilities I keep with me? Excess deceives suffering, don't you think¿ The white marks streaked across nothing's breast. I seek an unspeakable object. It's probably hidden in the most trivial holes. It should know I'm on the prowl. It hides in the uterus's stretchmarks. I move my hand between my thighs—I seek an unspeakable object—then up to my groin, the pubic hair around my pleasure has started growing again, thick, black, dirty, tangled. Some guys get off on hairy vaginas. I've let mine go to keep track of time. I use length of my pubes as a calendar. Mothers and whores know everything, they're omnipresent like the devil. They know every filthy inch of a man, he hides no surprises. His dirty nails, the warts on the soles of his feet watching over his sleaziest steps. They open their hearts; it stinks like open sewage. I'd pity the enemy who had to break bread with a man. I pity the wives that think they're better than whores. I pity the man who thinks he's better than a beast. I never cut someone a deal to suck a dick. And I've been sucked off for free. Nowadays, I'm one of the richest whores in town. I've always charged the price of gold. Golden pussy, that's what I'm known for around here, that and for my flair down there. You wanna see¿ I bet you do. I can show you later. Over there in the corner. Do you have a mirror with you¿ What for¿ You really can't guess¿ I want you to see It multiplied in the mirror. Have you ever felt what it's like to eat two pussies at once¿ I'll show you, I can make you feel it, and look, I'm just one person. I'm discrete, your bosses won't know. I already masturbated twice while we were talking and you didn't even notice. All I have to do is spread my legs, get in there, I'm already wet, soaking, lick my finger, take a taste. If you want, I'll hike my skirt up right here. Humanity's greatest invention was the skirt, don't you think¿ You want me to touch myself for you again? You'll see, it might even make you feel small. I've already swallowed up a lot of brave men with this thing here. You like women? You have the mustache of a guy who does, but if you want you can take me from behind, I like it like that. I've fucked plenty of faggots. No one is content with their patch of earth. Everyone wants to be the main character, but really they're just playing a supporting role. How many times have I choked on clumps of foreign soil, tripped on mushrooms from other pastures. I've slept with lots of geographers, too, they pass over every inch of your body calculating scales of measurement. I've helped them with their rulers and meter sticks, calculated the tremors that didn't occur, pilfered water from the reservoirs. I'm not getting off track, it's just that every discussion is vague and borderless, a sinuous geography. I've never found an answer when I've asked a question, things always fell into place after, like a tremor accommodating tectonic plates, with the typical listlessness of things, with the beautiful and brutal forgetting that comes with the seasons. With the rotting of the seeds that die swampy after heavy rains. Antonio Conselheiro swept lots of people into his flock. He wasn't pretty, you could even say he was ugly, but he had long hair like Jesus and on top of that he had a honey tongue. It's dark here, a cubbyhole world, a prison, a goddamned rattlesnake nest. The rocks are wet and they face us fearlessly, scraps of human skin adorn their crevices, their crickets, the crack is the rock's clitoris. I reach inside the crack, feeling for the G-spot. Some women wear rings on their necks, I pierce my labia with platinum. Grandmother, mother, father, cousin, brother, we all sleep together. We have no concept of incest, it died off along with the old civilization. At night the stench of carrion rises, of human femurs, of rotting guts. I can tell you there's hardly a difference between men, simians, and vultures, we're all hunting our next meal. We can't afford to pamper anyone;

everything's in short supply here and because of that we're animals. Did you know that scorpions will eat their own young when food is scarce? That doesn't faze you¿ Would you have the courage to eat your newborn's flesh¿ They say babies have tender meat because they haven't suffered yet, the only thing better than baby meat is angel. We all slept inside this dark cave. A clan. A globe in miniature. It was like he wanted to depopulate the world. A deadbeat nomad¿ Or was he a bitter cuckold¿ The most painful betrayal in history, that's what the shit-talkers call it, his wife ran off with a sergeant. After that he became a revolutionary, started wandering the world in search of comfort. Poor thing didn't know happiness is a loaded die, so he became an enemy of the state. But in our land no one knew anything of the hardships of society, we were a people ungoverned. Government was just a mirage, our territory had been given up to chance and that was how we liked it; destruction gave us autonomy. We were all born cangaçeiros. Without crime and without prisons. We removed many men's guts, perverted men who didn't deserve to live. We let the tripe dry in the sun, blacken the way you'd tan a bull hide—the ants came and did their part, all accomplices to the murder. So we were sure we were innocent. We were the judges and our ruling was never appealed. No good man had his skin cut or body pierced by a bullet. Death came for those chosen by God or the Devil. Inácio abandoned the people too. Inácio didn't speak, he only ever learned to sweep the property, grunting and rubbing his hands together like he was about to cast some powerful spell, even though his hands were as sterile as his butterfly brain. Stupidity is the worst of the martyrdoms. Around here men generally get their asses turned out at ten or eleven years old. His hands had probably never witnessed a climax, they weren't worth a damn, even to a chronic masturbator. He'd never sought out a whore to give him release, never lain with a woman or taken a man from behind. Around here men generally get their asses turned out at ten or eleven years old. Idiot said he was saving himself for a wife. He didn't want to be spoiled when he found the right girl. And there's no stain dirtier than a love stain. He got engaged to a bimbo from the other side of town. Things from over there provoke intrigue and hide secrets in closed fists. Little did he know that some mysteries are so cheap they keep scorpions in their pockets. Maybe the naive don't suffer. The wedding date was set, and when the judge arrived to officiate, the girl was fatter than a hog on killing's eve. She was pregnant and swore up and down it was the Holy Ghost's. Inácio gave thanks to God and praised Him for His blessing. After the first child came four more, all from the Holy Ghost and Inácio forever humbled to have been chosen. He started jerking off after that, since you can't desecrate a saint anyway. I spread my legs, offering to help, but he didn't even peek. Multiple times I tried to discover why he lived glued to the hem of that man's garment, but it was pointless, I scared him. He said I was a crazy witch without a hat, that I'd escaped the nuthouse and made a brothel out of a saintly village. I was happy with the title, even though I knew that whores had been born before God and that I wasn't at fault for anything. Either way, I've never been to a nuthouse but it's probably not much different than these crossroads, this dark sputum mixed in with the days' yellow dust. Sometimes I sit in the road splayed out like a dog, I chase the sun like my life hinges on the bestial act, I spread my legs and feel the wind and sand attack me, I take a piss right where I'm sitting, and it's ocher, hot, expansive, then, in that tiny manmade lake, I prod the earth and eat the nascent roots. It's like tasting your own beginnings, it's like discovering how your descendants will taste, it's like unravelling primitive beings by the navel, it's like digging up ancestral remains. I remember the brains of the primates I ate, the fit of the skull in my hand. I touch the antelope's hollow antlers and imagine them goring the universe's milky uterus in a raw and universal copulation. By eating dirt, I grow accustomed to the pit. The tastelessness of nothing. When I die my bones will rest in peace. Real corpses don't weigh on the earth. Their bones turn to dust, itching powder a spell in a witch's cauldron. I asked Gaguinho why he followed that crazy, hairy man with a big kisser and lots of friends who sniffs the ass of every guy he passes. Dunno, I don't ask questions. Not me, I'm quiet, zipped lips, horse hoof on my tongue. I'd talk more if life'd gave me a leg up. Can you imagine a life with legs, how funny'z'at? Aninha's look like flamingo legs, that animal that's all bright, you ever seen one¿ Boy did I like those legs, I'd spend hours looking at 'em quiet, but I never stopped to tell her how much I liked her stems. Maybe that's why I decided to start following Antonio Conselheiro, so I could see that slender body again and say how much I admire it. I worked my whole life and followed oafish men.

A spittoon for words on the floor. Guys who grind conversation with a pestle, eat hog's head, cow tongue, bull testes. No minced words, just chunks. Not much courtesy in the mask. Creating and fertilizing ill will just 'cause they're scared of leaking. Pretending that crying is a weed. A leaky man's a fruit loop. I've seen plenty of men mourn the bodies of other men, but I never seen 'em cry or moan. It's sad to have to dry out on the inside, like we're all taxidermied men. I touch my face and it's harder than an aloof donkey's face. Hard like a wooden sculpture, but if wood gets termites it goes soft, turns to dust when you blow on it, and mine's a big ol' dust pile. I know I lost my friends' respect; they think I turned fairy when I got old, some say it was defeat 'cause I lost Aninha. The truth is I didn't turn fairy, it's the opposite, I'm more of a man, less of a queer. They all kept polishing their hard masks, pretending their hurt ain't hurt. Not me, Antonio Conselheiro showed me the truth and I 'preciate him for that, weren't for him I'd still be that ugly rough-skinned lizard. But I do get a little sad 'cause I lost my reigns late, for a long time I looked at the world wide-eyed. You know what it's like to look wide-eyed at the world¿ It's like a fish who spent its whole life flying like a bird, a bird without lungs. I think it's beautiful when a man looks at the world from the corner of his eyes, sidewise, and, even still, sees it, and, even still, tells a long story, puts words in mute people's mouths, I've never met a storyteller character that wasn't also a teller of tall tales or a liar. The character of the storyteller who leers knows everything, knows the story of each pebble. Make-believe people have more tongue and saliva than men of flesh and bone. Now look at me, I'm a teller only of my own story and even then it's full of holes. A character on the other hand, he runs all over, wanders under the moon, under the hot sun and in the rain, makes friends with ghosts. He's got less teeth but there's gold in his mouth. More gusto with the carcasses. And he's got more courage, too, mounts an angry bull, shoots at crooks, disobeys the matador, evades the bullet. And here I am hunting pests in the rice field just for something to eat. Trapping forest critters. Tying up tomatoes so they don't fall over—it's sad to see a plant killed by the weight of its own fruit, like a woman that dies giving birth—digging a trench for the water to run, fleeing the snake's rattle, drinking pinga to cure the words gone to rot in the stomach. I bet you these ulcers of mine came from aborted words. But the pinga helped cure it, pinga cures everything, even a nasty flu. Sometimes I think I'm just a ventriloquist. This dumb doll director. A pretty word... Conselheiro explained what it was and I thought I'm kind of like that. A ventriloquist... hollow by nature. For a long time, all I knew was how to be a telegram, to give epitaphs, 'cause that was my job, I told relatives their relatives had died, we've never had telephones here. I didn't want to be like that, I wanted to know how to console. I wanted to talk nice, beautiful words in the middle, prepositions, conjunctions, although yet however but nonetheless. In my mouth words have the weight of an angry father, hickory switch whips wounding skin and pride. Giving bad news calmly was really all I knew how to do, that's why they called me. I'd be calm 'cause I stutter, the bad took longer sliding out the throat. Tears would flow. I'd start talking 'bout the difference 'tween pastures and green grass, 'tween silence and the sturdy knot only the dead can tie, of the dead that become saints, do miracles, of the lost souls still out there wandering happy. When they'd see me from far off they'd light candles, prepare the bed, the bath, the funeral clothes, the drink for the deceased. Sad for the families who can't prep and bury their dead. Words came out weak like a pinky finger or the last of an anemic cow's tit milk. But there were lots of feelings in my head; I guess they all turned to blood clots, knee injuries. Now I have to hold my nails back from clawing at the husk and making the thing bleed. I think I got it from my father. I'd hug him and it felt like he had a gorilla chest. You could learn 'bout evolution just by looking at him and so I started doubting God, not out of rebellion, just from observation. The thing that tells us it wasn't Adam and Eve, but that we started standing and becoming men. My father never finished the process, he only got halfway but they still gave him a man's soul. His face looked just like a monkey's. His huge hands like ancient tree bark. I tried to be less animal than him, but even still I can count on one hand the number of times I told Aninha how much I loved her. I regret it so, so much! She was so much taller than me she was hard to reach, my grunts didn't make it to her ears. For a while I thought maybe she was deaf, that's why she talked so bad, but that wasn't it, it was desperation, it was anguish because it was never women's turn. It was coffee with milk. One day, furious, Aninha shouted that what she really wanted was to be a whore, she should have been born a whore, because whores speak and they moan.

Whores thought, they were good at math, they did their books so they didn't get robbed and they cut lazy men with knives. Women were like dogs, they just didn't have tails because God didn't have the skill, they had to go through life kissing men's asses. I was gonna say it wasn't like that when she turned around and started stirring the big pan of preserves and I forgot to disagree. My spirit wasn't much for arguing. Also, she didn't talk much, always embroidering that same strawberry on the tea towel. And she was never done. It was so much abundance I got a little sick. I wanted to plant strawberries, but the weather was terrible and the strawberries got moldy and moldy strawberries are bad luck. On the towel the strawberries were alive and fleshy and never died. They were like a nicely tended crop, a rich person's garden. One day, by mistake, I tried to take a bite of one, tear out the flesh. Aninha shouted, said I was going crazy, trying to eat an illusion. No doubt the cachaça was eating my brain. Poor thing, she didn't know fantasy is the only thing that makes us happy. Makes us big, flashy, like meat drying in the sun. All the non-believers are dead now and the stench of their flesh don't reach our noses. You need a little lie to hold strong. Every suicidal person is a religious person waiting for God to forgive them. And God's busy with other things, like catching lice in children's hair. My head wanted to, but my head is hard and doesn't know clichés. I'm so happy now that I know all the quotes truckers put on the back of their sleepers. My mama always said she wanted to marry a trucker 'cause he'd tell her 'bout the truths she didn't know, bring her memories from the Holy City and seawater in a

Tubaína bottle. If she'd married a trucker, every day a new man would've appeared at her door, 'cause when a man leaves home and goes somewhere new, he turns into someone else. And she'd help him write the quotes and erase them and put up others. Mama never had a wedding, but she slept with lots of truckers. She'd say we can never attain a whole dream, we gotta be happy with half of one. She also slept with a fisherman. He put her nickname on his boat, but the boat sank right after. She never set down roots, though, she never gave in, didn't hiccup, she understood cartography and knew that the only thing people who stay in one place set down is ringworm, and ringworm eats away your solitude. One day mama took a giant atlas out from under the mattress, it was a present from Corisco, a cabra macho, a natural born killer. The atlas was all marked up with charcoal, each point was a place she'd visited in her head, wandering on the cheap, she used to call it. Mama tried to teach me 'bout scales, tropics, and imaginary lines. She knew the secrets of meridians and parallels, the zero mark and all those cartographic inventions that didn't get me anywhere except more and more lost inside; I thought there should've been some kind of imaginary line in our heads, that way we wouldn't get sidetracked so much. Greenwich, who could remember that¿ I never learned it, such a shame to be born on the back side of the globe, I always thought the world was too confusing to fit on a map. I never understood the compass rose. To me, when I walk backwards it's south, and forwards it's north. And the sun, well, it's not every day the sun sets in the west. She had magazines from faraway places stuck on the wall. She'd go to the market and when she came back she'd take the paper wrapping off. She knew there was a beautiful landscape in the middle of it all. She'd smooth those wonders she'd never visit out and tack them up real careful. Love was a fragile thing, a baby's soft spot. Lots of love wears out with the ugly screeching of doors. A gruff and agitated open-close then one day the thing jams, no one opens it anymore, not even an anemic little gap, not even that. Thing gets to rusting and ain't no one getting old rust off, man. The mouth went rancid. Grew moss. Dark-green-green. A geographic tongue. Guarded slumber, dude laid out at the entrance to the whorehouse. A drunk's morning breath. Piss and cachaça. I've lived almost eighty years, man, and I never seen anyone happy, I seen lot of people dying of sadness, but I never seen a man waste away from love. Women yes, I've met lots of women who cut it short once they got old, all because of passion withheld, but men don't withhold things, they don't hold in their wounds, they spread them. Every one I've met has only spread their hurt to me. Aninha never got love letters, how sad to never have gotten love letters, sadder than never getting love because in letters love makes itself so much more beautiful, so much more charming!!! A girl with makeup on, that's it, it's like a girl with makeup on, waiting. Now I've got my little scribbles, they're all there in a little yellow notebook, all for Aninha but Aninha's not here. Poor thing died of boredom 'cause I didn't know how to make the world told, the world was just a doodle to us back then, incomprehensible. I killed Aninha and I regret it! Aninha died drowned in my ignorance. One afternoon she took a chest out from under the bed. She opened it, looked at the embroidered strawberry cloths—they were at the bottom, giving shelter to the insects—and let the white roaches fly out the window. She sighed, she looked tired, her face looked like a night whose dawn would never break, the gaze on the back side of the page. She left. Died disillusioned by love and won't ever know that it was love she had inside her, that it was love when I stuck myself inside her, when I licked the door to her world, when I rang the bell she had near her groin, when I left my drool between her legs, when I rolled my cold foot over her foot hot from her socks and waited happy for day to break. When I brought back the biggest winter squash to make dessert, when I brought back copper pans all shiny and new. When she asked if the food was good and I said it's fine, least it'll stick to my bones. When I drank her coffee that was so weak it might as well have been potato water. She didn't know what love was 'cause telenovelas invented a bourgeois love I didn't know how to perform. Sad for Ana, sad for me, a stag without Ana. Tripping, falling all the time, scribbling and learning lessons of the heart that already went sour. Now, an immense clot in here causing me shame. If I knew how to prune right the roses would still bloom. If I'd specialized in grafting they'd be different colors, I'd invent Springs. They don't flower anymore. I seed and reseed the grass by her grave but nothing grows. You filled yourself with me, Aninha, and I am replete with you. When I look in the mirror I only see my opposite, and it's ugly, scary since you left, it's a strangled shout. If you'd had the genes of ruin, I would have said you left just to throw a tantrum. You ask why I follow Conselheiro, that's also why, 'cause of past deceptions. I liked the guy's face, his gentle ways. His leather sandals sliding, smoothing out the earth. The skin on his shins eating the dust. The sun exploding red on his back. You could count his ribs on your fingers and from far away, his body was slender like Jesus. I admire a man who only eats what he needs, gluttony is a vice I fall into often, it's not easy to forget those pulpy red strawberries, sometimes I puke just thinking 'bout them… Aninha was probably also half a saint, she made the absurd multiply, she was always stronger than me. I doubt there's a single woman who doesn't have wings on her back, men's turn to dust from so much happiness! I wish I had a full breast so I could feed the world. Conselheiro must have been born from a woman 'cause he was also strong. He carried a heavy cross like a saint. He spent his spit on the poor, explaining everything. The taste of the fruit borders the pit. If you pick it early it binds-gags the mouth. I don't understand his sayings but I think it's nice when people talk pretty. Tying knots in a tongue that's tattered and worn. The spiel starts to seem like a sculpture by that guy Carlinhos. ?Did you see the little angel he made? I wouldn't have been surprised if it sprouted wings and started flying. I don't understand politics. I follow him like I'm on a pilgrimage, wearing out what's left of my bones. A pilgrimage isn't a protest, it's a beautiful tomb to behold. I don't have living children, my girl died of boredom and monologue and I don't want to share her destiny, though I still dream of joining her. Death without company must be a drag, I don't like the idea of talking to myself for the rest of eternity, visiting the places I lived and not being able to be seen, looking at crops from a distance and not being able to kill the pests, seeing my friends and not being able to drink cachaça. Sadness wasn't made with us in mind, that's something for mangy dogs. When ticks get in the meat everything goes to rot. Dogs wake up with black guts twisted. Puppies are born with cords around their necks. I'll hop around while the leather still sticks to the bone. One day the revelry ends. God tears our fantasy away. I want a gentle death that comes child-like, on tippytoes, like a cat approaching the bed. When I open my eyes, night's dawn has already broken. Starless. Pitch, an empty sack of bread. Unguarded gallops. What will I do in the morning when there's no one left to listen to my dreams¿ Nightmare. The night's mare. Memories of the infanticide torment me, stop it, there's some desperation that's like a carcass, you have to bury it so the dogs don't find it. The longing almost killed me, I don't want it near me again, it's like a wallet-sized photograph, don't egg me on, that's a topic for another time. One day, when I'm on my way out, maybe I'll tell you how it all happened, but before that no, an oft-poked wound ekes pus, gathers flies, and some cuts deserve a good sewing. Don't insist or I'll fly off the handle. That's it, that's how it went with Guguinho and how it happened with most of them, just kept on keeping on for who knows why. People are waiting for something they find convincing, at least a little bit. Without conviction, why all this hallucinatory painting, these birds with nowhere to roost? This screen peopled with white. You can't show a man dressed as a saint to the poor. The whole town started losing its footing. The distance made the wind erase the way home. Fatigue rotted the steps back and the steps just kept on moving. So many of the devil's kin lost out there. But I stayed on, here. Without identity, feeble roots, a human tuber. The world is round, isn't that what they say¿ I won't wear my soles down just to come back with my tail between my legs. Wilted, fruit hanging off the stem. White guava once it gets maggots turns black. I resisted, I'm a woman with a lot of carcass. I don't get lost in the verses, the vague lines, the rondels, the crumpled paper's margins. My words are a straight line. I don't get lost in God's varicose legs. Men who talk in pretty rhymes hide evil in their souls. I have it on good authority that angels are mute, they don't have tongues or suffer from that evil. It was the dead who started getting chatty, forging trails. A sown seed that doesn't produce anything. The clothespins leaving tears in the wash left forgotten on the line. Calm down, there's no need to rush, this place doesn't abide by your logic, you can stay seated in your leather chair 'cause a dead cow don't moo. This land has its rules, its laws, its chronology, its margin, its mirror. Men who don't reflect here grow solitary, they aren't tying any neckties. Here snails are square and objects of worship. You ever seen a kid kill a slug with salt? It's so perverse to see time shorten in an animal's body. Are you real? I almost doubt your well-to-do dandy existence, it's so different from this hole. Did you look at the carcasses piling up out there¿ Why am I the only one who can see them¿ I didn't want to be born with so many watchful eyes. It must be my mom's fault, with all her witchcraft. It's better to stay on the edge of the bed. The gap between a dog's teeth is white. The most beautiful nights are those invaded by cannon fire, it's more beautiful than fireworks. No one ever heard of this war, but even so it must be painted in a portrait somewhere. Even a dead boy is beautiful in the hand of an artist. Lots of men lost their kids, their wives, their ears. My ear is still intact. I spend all day listening to bees buzzing on my left side. It's not enjoyable. A hive in my head. A paper wasp. A candomblé. Ants biting my brain. Yesterday I dreamed it was snowing in my mind. The acoustics of the void aren't very good, but I can definitely say they were blades. Dull, maybe that's why afterwards came the chatter, the shouts, the fibers gutlessly snapped. A stinking rag. It took so long—the scuffle seemed endless—that it really could have been a steak knife. Death doesn't scare me, the ritual does. Wringing a chicken's neck is crueler than shooting your dad. I hadn't imagined something so crazy, but now that you mention it, it is possible, it would explain a lot. I don't even know the victim, how would I know if they have enemies¿ I don't know a single man that doesn't have at least a dozen enemies. Do you¿ I don't think it would be useful to survey the property. This region doesn't leave fingerprints, plus, what good would the fingerprints of some unknown criminal be, some guy without a pot to piss in. A stillborn, as far as the world is concerned. There's tons of people like that around here, who don't exist in the system. ¿How many zeros to the left can mathematics go¿ Now I'm the only one around. In a sense that doesn't make me a suspect, it makes me a victim. When I showed up with eyes covered and hands bound, I noticed quick that the flowers here don't wilt, same as they don't bloom. A cemetery packed to the brim. I rubbed my hands together and shucked the seeds' potential life. The land was soft, almost flaccid, although there weren't rivers or streams nearby. Fat feet sank easy. A no man's land. The road was basically asphalt, the men didn't have enough courage to pour tar around there. The ground was so black on days with no moon that I really believed society ate and shat nearby. I couldn't get the bran or the smell of pigs out of my nostrils and my fingers got lost in their curly tails. The short circuits were never repaired. The posts never arrived. Life grew rarefied. I was a whore working the world's wide-open corner. The bottom of the trash barrel. All the cats were drab and didn't meow, they batted over cans looking for scraps, but the scraps had already been devoured by men. A few times I tagged along. Because I also know how to survive on what's no longer useful to anyone. If I'm still here it's because I wanted to see the insides from up close. Death without tragedy or representation doesn't provoke tears. Greek men invoking women with their phony masks, it still makes me laugh. A man is not a simulacrum of a woman, we are two separate species and the only thing that unites us is the spine in our backs. The news is vague and holds the fragility of human discourse. I'd smack the gum in my mouth and shove my two fingers in my teeth holes. My-mouth-my-pit. It calmed me down. Sometimes I'd grind my teeth. It was one of my favorite distractions, which ended up costing me greatly, since now my jaw clicks and unhinges while I'm kissing or blowing someone. I made it into my thing, an idiosyncrasy as the philosopher would say, I charged more for it, which, in a certain way, was ridiculous since gold wasn't worth a damn anymore. My meals are real symphonies. My skirt leaves two thighs exposed that at one point were thick and firm. Now, they're like two poorly made prosthetics. What matters is the red hollow—living flesh—dead mollusk without a roost scarfing the white gunk down. A crow copulating with a corpse. The white reproducing indecency. In all hands I carry brutality's scars. It's easier to breathe than to survive. Virgilio showed up on one of those nights, when the moon and desire were waning. One of those nights when there are more roaches than stars. One of those nights when agony is a wooden doll. I could tell his back contained a red sun that, despite being tired, never set... I didn't utter any words because I could tell by his expression that he was sick of small talk. Who hasn't asked themselves if staying quiet isn't better than idle chatter¿ I see a loose stitch on humanity's mouth-phlegm. I was also tired of pre-filling conversations with empty words, he didn't need to ask me, I would stay quiet, and anyways, my herpes was acting up, it wasn't hard to pretend to be mute. It was a lot easier for me to shut up, that way the insects couldn't mate on my tongue. I've already come off badly quite a few times from being tactless, not understanding. I wasn't interested in sticking my neck out again, so, the best thing to do was seek out the edge of a bed and rest until I was able to understand what was happening. I sat, crossed my legs, and waited. At some point he would say why he came.

And it didn't take more than two minutes. He ordered me to uncross my legs, stand up, rip off my clothes because he wanted love without nodules, without ribs, without bonds, without rushes. Rip it all off, quick, let's go, I can't wait anymore, look at my dick, it's hard, full, heavy, it's starving for your hot pussy. His eagerness got me going, I did what he said, and I won't lie, I liked it. After a few minutes he started to tell me why he came. He needed to feel the tenderness of new flesh, white and soft. He didn't want to touch me and feel bones poking through my skin. Look, look at my hands, they're all sliced up, they're bone chips. Surely he had me confused with someone else or was nuts. But I was too tired to argue or maybe I was already used to other people's insanity. What could a man like that want with me¿ I got scared, a fear I'd never felt before. What did he want, really¿ Did he not know where he was¿ Did he not know who I was¿ I was born with a festering cloaca. What did he want¿ When I was born, I already knew I was a whore. I couldn't hold my laughter in, it echoed off the four corners of the room, how could a whore know how to make love¿ Me, who judged men by the size of their dicks. Me, who was used to riding the horse's hard husk. Me, who's pissed on a few guys. How could any woman know how to make love knowing the weaknesses and perversities of men¿ There's a rotten moon in every man's face and you catch glimpses of the dark side. Women pretend, they've pretended since the time of caves. We pretend there's something more profound to men than the skin-epidermis-hypodermis that camouflages their bodies. We pretend we can find a sound that doesn't echo like a knock on hollow wood. We've pretended for centuries, but deep down, we know man's only function is the preservation of the species. Love is a silly idea to distract men's narrow and empty minds, I've never met anyone who's experienced it, just a few lunatics who confuse the feeling with mutual suffering. I made it very clear that I did my job like no one else, and that my job wasn't to love, it was to fuck, you don't buy love, it costs a lot, the shit's imported and I didn't know anyone in town who sold it. If he really wanted to find love he should look elsewhere, but I doubted he'd find it, I hadn't heard tell of the thing. And if anyone in that village had found love, they hadn't returned to tell the tale, they'd kept the secret for themselves. I lowered his pants and gave him a real nice blowjob because that was the consolation I was used to giving. Even though it smelled bad, the taste of his dick was remarkable. He sneezed his hot jet into my throat. I held the pasty liquid in my trachea for a while, it took it's time going down, I grew intrigued, I'd never felt something so dense that refused to come apart and, listen, I've tried everything. He confessed he was a poet <then I understood everything> hence the putrefied flesh and the bad smell, he hoped I didn't mind, he'd already tried every type of perfume but none could cover up the carnage. The smell bothered him, too, and it grew with the years, I haven't been able to feel anything for a while, and now I can barely sleep because of the horrible smell; I have terrible insomnia. It's awful to watch humanity sleep, to hold vigil over the bastards' rest while yours is absent. Poets change skin like they change outfits, I decompose all day, don't you see¿

My skin's peeling all over, poets are an incurable form of leprosy. Are you disgusted by me¿ I'm sorry, I didn't mean to scare you. Do you regret sleeping with me¿ I know, most do. By morning they're already asking me to leave. Don't worry, I won't be offended if you want me out of your bed, I know it's hard to handle the smell, but I'd like to stay, you know¿ Like I said before, your flesh doesn't have nodules or the ghosts of other times. Do you want me to leave¿ I didn't care, I'd already seen it all. Afterwards, he kept going like a crazy man, petting my skin, pawing at my tits, licking my pussy, shoving his finger in my guts, his fingers were like tweezers forged of desperation, he stuck them in, was working so hard he started sweating, it was like he was planning on ripping out what I had inside and throwing my tubes to the dogs. Then waiting for the pack to devour me. Don't be scared, my dear, I'm excited because you're the first pure woman I've ever fucked. I couldn't resist and let out another laugh, this time even louder, I waited and heard its echo in response, he was fucking with me, it was the only way. It was one of the dumbest things I'd ever heard, I almost kicked him out right then, I didn't like being made fun of. If he really wanted to stay, he shouldn't test my patience. He shouldn't have stupid opinions. A pure woman, me¿ You've got to be joking¿ Are you a poet or a comedian¿ Well, I don't really know what the difference is… Don't get mad, I didn't mean to offend you, you've got me all wrong. Right, I know it's not easy to see my reasoning, but I'll try, I'll explain what I mean by purity. You'll see that I'm right and I didn't mean to be flippant with you, quite the opposite, you're my chance at salvation, if salvation exists for anyone; I get the impression that we're all born condemned, that all of us are fucked and some more fucked than others. But let me get to the point, I got sidetracked, I'll explain to you what I mean by purity. I'm tired of fucking people who only want to fuck with me. I've taken beatings for no reason. My whole life, I've only fucked women with elevated souls. Women who recite Paul Celan, discuss dialectics, and can name every muscle that makes a smile. For a long time, I believed that was the only type of woman who could understand me, I thought that type of woman was less shallow in her soul. I was completely wrong, no one has ever been more wrong, I was victim of an erroneous theory of my own creation. You want to know what that got me¿ Nothing, absolutely nothing. I realized most intellectual women aren't much more than a slaughterhouse bull whose guts have just been ripped out. A bunch of stuffed beasts. Making love to a loved one brings the scorpions hiding in the holes to the surface. I didn't want to have slept with the ones I loved, much more preferable to sleep snuggled up with my worst enemy, waiting for the knife to go in. Only the ones who love you can take you to hell, make you take a stroll around, bring you face to face the devil. I can't reach climax with all that bitterness coursing through my dick, my memory; my dick remembers, and I have the memory of an elephant, you know¿ With you it's different, your body, your sex is virgin to me, your flesh is soft, it doesn't have nodules from other times, no grooves or scars. I can sleep in your lap and not fall into abysses or off cliffs. I can offer my dick to your mouth and know that it won't be butchered, I can offer all my extremities and know that none will be amputated. I shove my tongue between your legs and know that the liquid gushing out won't be acidic to the point that it eats me away. You know, there was a time when I was forgetfulness, but, little by little, I started losing interest in the things that made me human, I'd observe night's hanging gills, the reptiles' dead skin... sometimes I looked a lot like a lizard, other times I'd transform into a frog, a tadpole, I'd hide my anxiety and run my hand across my head, and it would cave in from the fissure caused by time's trepanation, I'd touch my belly and notice that each day the size of my intestines shrank drastically, and after a few years I wasn't much more than a gutted fish in spawning season, an empty being, forgotten on the river's muddy banks. You probably don't know what that means, nobody does. Have you ever seen a gutted fish¿ Those fish men fish, they tear out their guts only to realize they're too small, that they wouldn't even feed an insect, they think they're not worth taking home, not worth hauling off in the sack with the others, so they toss them aside and there they stay, dead on the muddy riverbank. I'm one of those little fish, I never learned to swim in a school, I became what you see now, this soft thing, stinky and useless. If I at least was a breeding bull, one of those strong black sires, but I wasn't even capable of that. All that babbling irked me, I didn't ask for an explanation, I hated them, a whore doesn't need anything clarified, the details of his anguish pissed me off, that useless cerebral ejaculate, plus, it reminded me of that idiot philosopher, I didn't see much difference between poets and philosophers, neither could keep a boner while their brain was working, both mixed pleasure with bibliographic citations, tried to impress with the feeble exactitude of words. Neither understood that words are dead or that a tongue in your crotch is worth more than a whole grip of worthless lexicon. He waited a few days to leave, said that his body was lifeless and he needed some time to recuperate. He'd also hurt his leg, he'd been walking for days before he showed up and his wound was worse for it, it wasn't anything serious, but he needed to rest before walking again. Can I stay here¿ I understand if you don't want me to, I don't want to force you into anything, it's just that there aren't any houses around here. I don't need much, any corner will do, I can sleep on the floor or with the dogs. I didn't put up a fight, I said he could stay as long as he wanted if he paid me, I didn't like doing favors, even less so for strangers, that would make a weak woman out of me, plus, I didn't want him to think I was his lover, it wouldn't be good to get things mixed up, I didn't want to be a lover to anyone who talked that much, someone who spent hours circling around his own center. I also made it clear that he would clean up his own mess, especially those hairs that kept falling off his body, they might scare off the other clients. That was my daily bread, I couldn't get sidetracked by every guy who showed up asking for help. I wasn't running a hostel. It wasn't anything personal, it would be the same for anyone who asked to stay. No man had ever had the courage to ask to stay with me there, the ones that stayed over, stayed to fuck; I guess you could say he was my first houseguest. He agreed to everything, he seemed happy to be able to stay on neutral ground, and on the nights that followed I bore no witness to his insomnia. During those days, I started to understand a little about love's difficulties. He told me horrible stories, some real—some he witnessed himself or participated in actively—others fictional, but as he himself said, sometimes fiction is crueler and truer than reality. I enjoyed those days, distracted by his fantastical stories. I began to notice how much love was like a chained-up dog. A feathered dog, but one that couldn't fly. I felt bad for lovers. I felt bad for me. I was also a small fish, but I pretended I was schooling to escape the crowd, I keep moving onward, my scales have always fooled the idiots, in fact they've been my greatest defense. It's not easy keeping your eyes open and saturated in the rocks. We pay dearly for not having grown eyelids. We're protected because we see everything, every minuscule detail, every proton breaking loose from the nucleus and we're cursed because we see everything, every minuscule detail, every neutron breaking free from matter. We're cursed because we weren't denied sight. After a month of rest the wound on Virgilio's leg closed, the skin was still a little thin and smooth, but he had recovered. He gave me a kiss, thanked me for the pure love I had given him, thanked me for the accommodations, took a reasonable amount out of his wallet and placed it on the bed. I went to take the money but quickly realized how ridiculous it was, I charged out of sheer force of habit, money was no good anymore. I straightened my back, which had already hunched slightly toward the mattress, extended my hand and garbled a goodbye. He said maybe he'd come back some day, maybe he'd find a town besides this one, maybe he'd raise goats, he heard they still exist in huge numbers in some regions, maybe he'd acquire a plot of land, maybe he'd raise horses, maybe he'd write a book, maybe he'd kill a man, maybe... and he listed so many hypotheticals that I was sure I'd never see him again. Once you've lived long enough it's easy to figure out that maybe means never or don't count on it, babe. When Virgilio left, I'll admit I felt a little sad, even though there'd been no laughter at all during our goodbye, in some ways his smell, as the days went by, had stopped bothering me, and I thought that living with someone is a lot like having an ingrown toenail, it feels pretty bad, but you get used to it. I didn't have a choice, I cut the toe off. A few months later I couldn't understand why I'd been sad, after all, there's no company more perverse than that of a man and the exhaustion it entails, even more so a man with a heinous pact with words. That afternoon I started thinking that sometimes we make knee-jerk and pointless decisions, and for a moment I was satisfied with being cold-hearted. It wasn't long and the man that I wasn't waiting for arrived. Love blooms in Spring. He carried a medallion with these stupid sayings and if it hadn't been for his commonplace face, I wouldn't have given him the time of day. But there was no way such an ordinary face could go unnoticed. He looked cheesy, like one of those guys who pretends to be rich and important but doesn't have a pot to piss in. Black mustache slicked with spit, white shoes and tie. Gold chains. I'd have sworn that one day he'd die of love like in a Mexican soap opera. Like in the love stories that happen every day in the gutter, on dark paved roads. Like the children conceived and aborted in foul-smelling alleys. But I knew: happy love makes terrible books, the pages' dirty ears multiply in the universe's fingers. There wasn't much difference between dawn and dusk. Solstice-Equinox in my vague body. A loose planet. A dead plant. A red moon / A sunset on my coccyx. The eye-conscience of the asshole. He had swagger, he could hold love like he held berries, shake it, watch it do a two-step and take a piss in his hands. He could do whatever he wanted because he'd been born old and was good enough he could pull one over on the Devil himself. And he used all his smarts to con the whores around here, but what he couldn't imagine was that in these parts it's Fall all year round, and that's, maybe, why passion never blooms. You'll find that's why the few whores I knew around here were sad and had huge bags under their eyes. Dry yet still fruiting fig trees. There's no bigger turnoff than a whore that's sad. I'd rather die than sigh sadness out my pussy. Only Latinos write stories where whores are decent, sad, and loving. I've never met a slut that didn't love fucking more than anything in the world. And now I'm here, alone in this hole, fighting ants for space. No one to fuck. One day I manifested that I'd fall in love with the first man who treated me good. Or with the first one who didn't stick anything in my pussy but his dick. That's how I fell in love with a machinist. It's hard to believe that a machinist would be lively, it's like they're all just part of a train, another piece, another fitting. I liked how he operated my body, searching for gears to ruin me with. I genuinely don't know where he came from, it had been two hundred years since the trains stopped running. Maybe he only operated trains in his mind, sometimes desire and reality get confused, and vice versa. Looking through the gap, you can still see a few carcasses. After he left, I never fell in love again, I spent every day watching the carcasses being nibbled by the earth, a special kind of sunset over the ruins. What was surprising was that he was barely thirty and had the best dick I've ever seen. And he didn't need anything else to make me happy. I suspect no man does, I suspect happiness only exists between our legs and doesn't last longer than an orgasm. I'm even more suspicious of multiple orgasms. Every man that hasn't known how to fuck me has made me unhappy. We spent weeks on end locked in the bathroom. I got to know the depths of every corner of that room, and I came in all of them. The moist, acrid smell didn't bother us. He'd spit on my sex then penetrate me, first from the front then from behind. The mold on the walls spread, the lizards multiplied then plummeted from lack of space; they formed a sticky mat on the floor and our bodies simultaneously grew slippery like frogs, which made it easier for them stick together. The latch grew rust. It was like that for three months. And maybe things wouldn't have changed if he hadn't gotten that attitude, but I don't blame him, it was necessary. I was never bored during that time. The mycoses made my skin whitish, but I didn't care. The humidity made my hair grow fungus and fall out. I didn't care about that either, it wasn't my mane that distinguished me from men, it was my amputated penis that set me apart. One day he got offended, scrubbed the floor with his tongue, drank urine, ate his own feces, scraped off the husk that had taken over the surface of his skin, dug the ditch a little more, searched for water, killed the critters hiding in the corners, removed the scum from the walls, ripped the ingrown nails out with his teeth, imprinted his teeth in my back, he couldn't contain himself, he grew fat, broadened his shoulders, stuck his cock out, the whole thing barely fit in the tiny latrine. Then he cleaned off the rust, spat inside my mouth—not on my sex—unlocked the door, and left. I let out one last moan, no longer from pleasure, although I did masturbate as he walked away, I'd gotten used to easy love. Before leaving, he handed me a dagger and said love and tango pierce the flesh, and if we don't pay attention, they'll go all the way to the bone. Don't think I loved you. If you're thinking that you're wrong, crazy even. Listen here, I didn't love you. I couldn't be capable of loving you. No man can love a whore, even an idiot knows that, you knew it when you sucked me off the first time. I couldn't stop you, what man could resist? Man's weakness is his dick. I know you liked it, I did too, but this can't go on, I have better plans. My life can't amount to a single eternal fuck. Men love their wives or other men. I don't mean to say I didn't have a good time, I had a great time, but I got sick of watching the moon depart and the sun arrive the moon depart and the sun arrive and the moon depart. You told me yourself the day-to-day is tedious and puts a hair up our asses, when every day is the same it's like watching the same movies on repeat. I didn't hear you because I was fucking you, but now I see you how right you were, I was the one with shit for brains. I want something else, routine's not a good accessory for a whore, you should have been smarter. A whore is a whore. You should have sent me off, let me fuck you then sent me off, kicked me out, it would have made more sense given your profession, but instead you kept letting me stay and I started not believing you. A whore is like an old car you like taking for a spin every once in a while, but eventually you pass it off to someone else. I agreed with him, I didn't like arguing. I couldn't live my whole life locked up in a bathroom having sex, even if I still think fucking is the only genuine activity, the clitoris doesn't lie, you can fake a moan, but not the desperation of the vulva contracting and begging for more. I still dream about that dick. I awake at night's center, on the edge, and have to touch myself. I lock myself in the bathroom. I drag my tongue across the wall, spit, and use my finger to mimic his dick. A sizeless darkness, implausible, visible only to the blind. I ferreted through sewage. The shit smelled good to me and it wasn't immiscible, quite the opposite, I was made of that same airy material. I was fond of dogs and brown cats. Lions were rare. It was during those hours that I discovered I had been abandoned in the middle of nothing. A few minutes before, I was in the moist darkness of my bathroom, and then there I was, splayed out in some strange space. There was no sound, no shuffling, no noise, it was like I was trapped in impossibility. Given that my ear got me nowhere, I tried to see, but even my eyes were useless there. I looked around and tried to recognize where I was. Nothing was familiar, it was all thoroughly new, a clear and schizophrenic new. I thought maybe it was just a nightmare, or who knows, maybe after masturbating I'd slipped in the bathroom, hit my head, and gone into a coma. But that seemed unlikely, I had no bruises, and plus, I was completely awake, I wasn't unconscious at all, my thoughts were still in order and things were happening chronologically, nothing like the imprecise sequence of dreams. I tried to find other explanations for the state I was in, but none of them fit. I breathed deep and tried to calm myself down, maybe things weren't as bad as they seemed at first glance. I dug through my memory, retraced my mental steps from the moment I woke up until I got to the bathroom—that didn't get me anywhere either. I still had no idea how I'd ended up there. The plan was to forget about it and wait for sleep to come, but I tried and failed for half an hour, so I thought I'd try getting up. I couldn't, it was like something sticky was keeping me on the ground. I sought out my fingers, they tingled like they belonged to someone else's body. I remembered that before blacking out I'd touched myself, so I tried to lift my hands to my nose to see if I could still smell myself, maybe I'd been there for days and hadn't noticed. But even though my hands weren't bound, I couldn't move them. I was desperate and started thrashing around as hard as I could. There was no way, someone had to be nearby watching me, but why¿ Why me¿ What did they want from me¿ I didn't have anything to give, anything! It couldn't be sex because I wouldn't even deny a homeless person the pleasure. I couldn't wrap my head around what was happening, part of my face was paralyzed, too. I tried to move the other part and felt it respond to my efforts. I tried the same with my leg and it also reacted. I don't know what they gave me, but half my body was dead, only half of me responded to external stimulation. I saw some white powder to my left, which I quickly recognized as cocaine, of course it could also have been a little salt, but I liked the first idea better. I thrashed violently, until my healthy side managed to grab some of it. I needed to snort it, needed to snort a lot to survive, my body craved numbness, my pores needed relief. And that's exactly what I did, I snorted it, I railed that white powder. By that point I couldn't even tell what the substance was, it had been a long time since I'd seen cocaine—it was highly unlikely it was cocaine. At this point, I'm almost positive it wasn't, it had to be some other type of narcotic, since I didn't do much more than sleep badly, a rest that lasted for nights on end. I had horrible nightmares, I tried to wake up but couldn't, my cries didn't make it past my mouth. I spent days there, I vomited on the ground without being able to move. Little by little the paralysis improved and I started to tingle, indicating that soon I'd be cured. By then I was done fighting it, I laid there until the paralysis had completely worn off. Something like ten days must have passed before I was able to get up and look around. But there wasn't anything to look at, it was all deserted, there was no one there, it was a small room without windows, furniture, or plants. To the side of where I had been lying was a half-full bucket of water. I bolted out of there, I had to flee as fast as I could. I walked forever, really, but I didn't find anything but a creek. There was nothing else I could do, I had to return to the small empty room, at some point I'd have to remember how I got there, and until I did it would be impossible to get out. I had no idea what side of town I was on. In the days that followed I was locked in there, and when the water ran out I had to walk for kilometers to get more—good thing I had already found the creek, I still didn't know where the river was but it couldn't have been far, and anyways who needs a river or an ocean if you've got a creek¿ I got in the habit of putting the bucket on my head < I'd seen it in the movies, a long time ago, before the war > because that made it easier, heads are stronger than arms. For months I tried not to comprehend why I was in that situation or who had put me there. I walked around the place all day, that way when night came I had no trouble sleeping. On one of those nights, I heard animals roaring, rodent sounds, men arguing, and beating on the ground, I stayed quiet, pretended I was dead. Even now I don't know what happened, I felt a blow to my neck, and when I woke up I was in my bed at home, and an old client was knocking on the door. I didn't have time to think about how I'd gotten there. I was just a woman, a whore but a woman, we're not used to thinking, we get by on intuition alone. If not for that I wouldn't have survived the first sack of shit who socked me in the face. After a few years I got used to it. It was nice to see men subjugate other men. It was more than nice, even just a little and I'd get excited. My asshole was already primed for easy pleasure. I couldn't watch a man ripping another man's guts out without coming close to climax, I'd feel the liquids start flowing and spritzing my pussy. It was good to see the limits of others' pain, to slowly tally the compound fractures, the dislocated shoulder.

Violence gave me goosebumps, made my hairs stand on end, it made me wet, I'd put my fingers between my legs and they'd be soaked so I'd bang one out right there, first with three fingers, then a cock to finish me off. I liked seeing the victim suffer, I wanted him to compare the scale of his suffering to the bounty of my pleasure. A few times I even ended up riding the reject. I'd lie on the ground, light a cigar (in those days they didn't have a nationality, they didn't need to be Cuban, they just needed to burn) and I'd sit there watching lustfully, sometimes I'd stick my fingers between my legs again and work on my pompoir skills while I smoked. I didn't have a cock, but even so I felt like I was hard. Must be that phantom limb thing. I've had so many dicks inside me I've basically had a penis before, I've peed standing up. The piss dribbling near the zipper. The music was low. I couldn't quite tell what it was. Jazz, maybe. Yeah, true, I could have imagined it was jazz because it's the music I like. Whores sometimes like to hear a nice tune while they're fucking. I liked it, I'd even moan along with the sax. I would also get off to Bergman films. Before the war, that is, before all the cities were destroyed. Now our pleasures are others, much different, more limited, we have to struggle to eat, fight over a chunk of meat, debase ourselves. Even so I'm not just some woman. Each sole leaves a mark without equal where it steps. I'm a 37. I liked to play it in Jogo do Bicho. It was my lucky number. Ever since I've known Rámon, every number is his lucky number, I've never seen anyone make a buck at cards that wasn't him. Rámon was quite the bookie, and a whore. It was easier to trust a thug than a good-for-nothing.

He had the smoothest game in town, give him five minutes and he'd convince you of anything, then take your clothes off to boot. Occasionally he'd disappear, only to return with next to nothing, thinking he could buy me for chump change, but I didn't sell myself for scraps. Sometimes I'd accept the objects he offered me so I didn't offend him, because aside from being worthless, he was also very nice, it was impossible not to let him butter you up. He'd bring objects from an antique store, which, according to him, was a family heirloom, one of his sisters watched it while he was away. He said that before the war he was rich, that he had women lining up to marry him, but he fucked them all then tossed them out because he didn't like gold digger love. I found the story hard to believe, Rámon's face held the marks of poverty, it was obvious he'd never been rich, but after the war, everyone who survived tells the story they want. I also found it hard to believe the part about the antique store, but who knows, maybe there's another world outside this one, maybe other cities survived the catastrophe. Nothing made more sense than a store for odds and ends and these days any odd or end could be called a collector's item. Rámon was slippery, he'd even trade his mother for a lampshade, if he had one, that is—he was birthed from an incubator. There was no way that thing had grown inside a belly, best case scenario it was the belly of a horse. When I was hard up, he'd pay me and settle for a blowjob, as long as I swallowed hungrily, and I knew how to fake it like no one else. If a woman has any advantage over a man, it's her ability to fake desire. Women have only gotten this far because we can fake it, if it weren't for that we'd have been wiped out ages ago. I didn't have time to think anything. I know I didn't recognize the face I saw between the slats, if I'd seen it before I'd have known. He definitely isn't from around here, if he was, he wouldn't escape. Let me tell you: there are two things I never forget, a face and a cock. I hate hypotheticals, this one-way trip is hypothetical enough. A machine, a camera, I don't know, a kaleidoscope, maybe? A film without a screenwriter. It was dark in there—a kissing bug a childhood ghost—but that's irrelevant. Rhizomes direct us away from the verdant trunk. The sap reminds us of milk from ample breasts. My mother's breasts were dry and it was bad enough you couldn't pray it away. Hunger makes us overly imaginative. Invention is the weapon of the weak, that's why I hate fiction writers and philosophers. I never met a degenerate that wasn't a fantastic storyteller. Silence is for the soulless. Missing teeth stokes the fantasy. How many beautiful mouths have I seen losing themselves at cheap orgies. What's in the spotlight can be clearly seen. Skylight. That's how I witnessed many crimes. That was how I killed lots of dirty beasts hidden in the clarity, by disguising myself as darkness. Sometimes men forget they're also beasts, that they can dig a hole to hide in while the storm passes too. Criminals forget we can see what's in the light from the darkness, but that the inverse isn't true. That was also how I came to try the strange taste of human flesh for the first time. The taste, the texture. The vein giving your teeth the slip. The marrow cascading from the corners of your mouth. I never thought I'd sample a member of my own species, but what's worse, I never thought I'd like it so much. There's only one thing I can say compares to the sensation of chewing a man's flesh. What was it¿ The feeling I'd get when I snorted a couple lines of coke then got on a dick. Do you really find cannibalism that unacceptable¿ I don't think it's absurd at all, man is a beast like any other, with the caveat that you have to remove the toxins before you dig in. Has anyone ever gone so far as to eat their own fetus? It's a ritual in a few neighboring tribes to devour-annihilate the firstborn. What's so shocking about that, really? How many animals have you devoured with all the refinement of a civilized man? Our tendency towards indignation is comical, it's almost a memorized prayer, a litany, but there's no real indignation, it's an apparatus, we have no real capacity for scruples. Admit it, you, like me and like the others <those over there that revel in grinding up the bones> you would eat the meat too if you were in our place, you would deal a deadly blow for a bigger cut, too, you would fight other living starving beings for the flesh of the dead, too. Come on, don't be ashamed, I get you, I'm not going to scold you, if you want you can whisper it right here in my year, I like dirty secrets. Around here we don't care much for good manners, good habits ruined men's instincts, made them dummies, an extinct species. You really are a coward! You're just like the others, can't take a dump without lying about it. Don't expect me to help you out by giving you my story, you're getting on my nerves. So that's how it is, I'm the only one who has to play ball¿ And why would I play ball with you¿ What am I getting out of it¿ You know what, I'm not getting shit and I'm not opening my mouth again, if you want to know figure it out yourself. You don't see things that way¿ You think you're all high and mighty, you're just a mosquito slurping a pile of shit. The flies stay still, dropping the same eggs in multiple wounds. Up close you seem so hypocritical! So you want to pretend that looking in my crossed eyes (in this world you have to rip out the fish's guts and throw a dart at the cat at the same time) you never noticed that every day men eat each other, just like the scorpions with their cannibalisms and their heads up their own asses¿ I've heard so many beautiful diatribes but they've never been tied to action. Men are devoured and we don't hear a peep, it's like we're insects, invertebrates. Locusts destroying crops. An insipid agglomeration of cells. The lower part of the extremities. No doubt it was made of titanium. Or some other impenetrable material. Only thoughts are porous and ideas liquid. You could recognize them by the clack of their steps and of their kicks. Steel boot. The sons of bitches have great aim. They know how and where to hit and what they don't have is the shakes. That's not important anymore. No one cares about details, I don't care. Idiots and poets are the ones losing time on minutiae, searching frantically for the perfect comma. The majority think in arroubas. Keeping note of each blow, the thighs ever purple. The round thigh (fat weighs more than nerves)*** atop the white bone conceals all carnage. That which I've already kissed-nibbled-hawked up. I scribbled

*** Some new scientists are attempting to prove that the weight of fat differs by 0.0001 grams from the weight of nerves. Orthodox scientists don't admit such absurdities.

names, made annotations, infamous books that faded away after a bath, Sade's mania. I spat each word in your filthy ear. You'd say my dirty talk excited you as I rode your hips. You weren't the type to find happiness in a pussy, you were a resentful man and would die waging war with your own ghosts, cursing the victories of others. Nothing made you happy or even satisfied. I should have noticed how stupid I was being, but I didn't. I didn't trust men, but you were indifferent and that fooled me. No, I wasn't in love, but there was something about you I found intriguing, and I had to follow you. What would I do after¿ I don't know, I could have made love to you as much as I could have shot you in the forehead. When night came I liked to run my hands along your spine and watch you arch your back like a cat. I was too human for your abstractions, your thoughts were fat, obese, I couldn't believe they came from that puny body, almost anemic, almost Kafkaesque. No one had ever seen you emotional. Your face was white and had no features, a wax doll. A few times I'd run in silence, following your tracks. I'd hide my slim body behind the sparse trees. During those hours I was terrified I'd get caught red-handed. How would I explain myself¿ What would I say¿ That I was following him out of childish curiosity¿ No way he would believe me, he'd demand complex motives and my motives were vile. I breathed deep so I wouldn't run out of air and have to call for help. If I fell flat on my back out there in the middle of that desert he'd see me, I don't know if he'd come to my aid, but I would be unmasked. The dry air made it easy to pass out and lose your senses. I didn't want to pass out, I didn't want the crabs to eat me alive. I heard a story about a man who got lost around here and eaten alive, with no one to help him. He never saw me or he pretended he didn't. He said that men would only make sense if they could camouflage themselves in the hardness of rocks. He'd sit on the rock, next to the vast carcass, and eat the heads off the fish. Only the sizeable ones, the others he's toss back into the sea as if they hadn't earned the privilege of being bitten by him. I watched him gloomily, distantly, while those animals' brains were annihilated and their bodies, intact, piled up beside the sea. Before biting into them he'd say a few words, but it was impossible to make them out from afar. Then, before sinking his teeth in, he'd suck the head until the sockets came loose. It seemed to me that if he stayed there for another hour, all the animals would go extinct and the sea would transform into one giant, dead school. My eyes hurt from looking at the fallen scales to his right. My wounds stank more than those ruined fish. He was a bad man and that didn't offend me. He wasn't a man of nuance, I'd never met or sucked off one that was. One day he asked me to close my eyes and open my hands, he had a present. I was surprised, I didn't think he was capable of nice gestures, I thought he only knew how to ask, but I was wrong. I closed, opened my eyes and saw a blue scorpion walking towards my arm. I said nothing, no gesture of gratitude, he smiled and asked if I liked it. What could I say¿ I didn't want to offend him, it was the first time he'd been nice since he showed up in town, I didn't want to hurt his feelings. I stayed silent and watched the scorpion scale my breasts, it circled around them, didn't know the secret of females, and it wasn't long before it was lost in the hairs of my pelvis. I didn't insult him, I waited for it to graze my clitoris, let out a small groan, it fell, and then I stepped on it, I felt its shell crack, it was the middle of the night, which meant the sun would soon devour the rest of its body. I don't know why I did it, I didn't want him to think it was an insult to the present he gave me. He looked in my eyes for a long time, he was sad, he let out a grunt and then he left. I didn't shout, didn't ask him to stay, I knew that he wasn't where he was supposed to be; he wasn't from here, he wasn't from anywhere, he didn't belong to any species. He was a hybrid, he was wandering and would continue to do so until he died. He would never adapt to our way of life, we don't have space for lunatics here. I would have liked to have been able to help him, but I couldn't, I was a flying fish and he would never be able to cut off and eat my head. In the philosophy of the hole there are no fancy words. A dick is a dick and it's wielded like a combat weapon. There are no women, it's the old problem of the human harvest, men would rather fuck other men to avoid reproducing and having to share their bread. Even though most of us weren't nomads anymore, we still had our rules, it was the only way to survive scarcity. Me, I was the last refugee. I was a vagina to them. When they got tired of fucking each other they'd seek me out. They'd pull my hair by the base then pump one out impiously. Sometimes I'd respond to the attack with long moans. They'd spit right after. They were satisfied, that much was clear. I was good even when I was passive. The blood and spit cooled off the shapeless middle of my hips. Many worlds have plummeted from that basin. But then they grew distant and couldn't even remember where they came out of. A huge, vague vulva casts a shadow over my head. We never remember. The first soil we bring to our mouth smells like disgrace. Every nightfall calls putrid bodies to the door. Every balled-up fist seeks a belly for relief. A sunset to tease out-rip open. Who can swear they never thought of stabbing and fucking their mom? Tonha, my mother's name, contained the disgrace of old age. You didn't need to get close to see she was born old. Her feet touched the ground first, like an aloof beast, and only later did they dig her head out the uterus. That's why she was kind of, you know, on the moon; that's why the craziness took her. The only things she knew by heart were prayers and the names of roots, but not even that could keep her from sleeping with a bunch of guys. She was weak, she didn't believe men were capable of sustained passion. They left their women before their bellies started to swell. She slept with lots of men before my father, but all of them left. I have lots of siblings out there. I don't know anything about them and they know nothing about me. Sometimes I figure I've already slept with a few of them. ¿How would I be able to tell? Men are all the same, except when it comes to the size of what's between their legs. Plus, it can't be incest to sleep with a half-brother you don't know. I didn't know my dad. He was a big man, he ate with his glazed eyes fixed on his plate. He was straight, direct. He tilled the earth with such focus that even the worms would jump up scared, they'd hop around severed in two. But you know how women get when they fall for a man, baby girl, they can't get a grip 'til they've licked his pecker. And one woman's happiness is a million other women's shame. I begged him to stay, to forget those perfect asses, 'cause it wouldn't be long before they got big enough to deepthroat the world, women don't stay pretty for long in the company of a man. Soon enough her hard tits would be dangling off her chest like a couple rotten fruits. And her pussy wouldn't always have the sweet aroma of youth. What he was living was an illusion that was soon to end. I knew men, they were easily impressed by beauty, but beauty never got them anywhere. I begged again, got down on my knees, ripped his pants off with my mouth, I licked his cock like I'd never licked it before, but he didn't even care, he shoved me off and called me a slut, said a real woman would take the insult standing up. He ended up leaving with Flor. I did everything I could to stop it, but he was blind. She was a looker, with her soft, delicate skin. Her eyes begged time to rape her, and time, well, he accepted. Flor came back three years later with two wilted children under her arms. Said their father had run off to the woods. Didn't want anything to do with women anymore, women were the devil's work, all they did was mess with men's heads, throw them off course. A woman wasn't worth fucking. Mom said poor thing, but I saw in her eyes that she was happy Flor had also gotten old and grown wrinkles around her mouth, she was a cistern of wounds. Her pussy had grown moss. Poor thing, I'm sure it's hard to find a man now. What man would want to run off with a saggy-mouthed mossy-pussy woman¿ Who knows, men are a strange breed, rarefied, they don't cast a shadow and it's hard to guess what they're capable of. A scorpion moves the wall, the same scorpion that tormented Lorca in the nineteenth century. I don't pick fights with any of them, they're slippery like frogs. What's for damn sure is they weren't made to please a woman. I learned quick that love is a luxury item you buy in a boutique. Love was invented out of boredom. We got bored, created monogamy, then labelled the neurosis a loving feeling. The same body that grates gives us pleasure. A fine ware. A lady fills her mouth to say she loves it, they'd found the right man, as if men were born to fit our measurements, as if men were capable of being born, of rupturing animality's husk. The others had litters like rats, and they were ugly little beasts. One litter after another, rats of every color. And all Paris was to them was the name of an off-brand perfume, a boil, a cyst. Maggoty meat. As for me, I'd never let a strange beast gestate inside me. My body wasn't made to house another body. I'm not maternal, a kid only drags you down. A child is a loogie you forgot you swallowed that ends up sliding out your pussy hole. I'd rip it out with my hands right here if I could. I'm not scared or pious, those feelings only affect the weak, and mine is a noble, aristocratic spirit. I don't know how I could've been so damn careless, I could have avoided the entire headache, you're right, it's not the first time it's happened, but I managed to take care of the others on my own, just me and my knitting needles. I don't know what happened this time, I bled and bled and the damn thing was still up there, toying with me and my patience. I had to get help. I went to the midwife, the one who brought things into the world and also took unwanted children out of it. I didn't know what else to do, I'd already drunk all the teas and performed all the rituals I knew and there it stayed, swelling my hips and belly. It was strange, so small and already so full of its own ideas. It had taken over my body, a parasite that moved in without asking permission then refused to leave. I already hated it and it wasn't more than a bean. No bigger than a bean and already getting on my nerves, messing with my sleep schedule, I didn't rest for weeks. My eyes were heavy and felt like they were ready to leap out their sockets at any moment. My belly moved around like the fetus was at twenty weeks already. I'd never seen anything like it. I'd been around pregnant women since I was young, but their bellies only ever started moving around the fifth month. Smells made me sick, even fucking was too much to handle. I puked every morning, I couldn't keep anything down, the little creature was nauseating, that's what it was, nauseating. This woman was my only way out. The hallway was dark, dirty, and smelled like death, but I didn't care, I waited for hours, I guess no one in town was enjoying motherhood. I looked at the faces of the other women waiting on the benches, they had every size belly you could imagine. Is this your first time¿ Yes, it is. The big-bellied woman let out an evil laugh and her belly leapt and laughed along with her. Are you scared¿ I'm not scared of anything. You're not scared of going into that operating room and never coming out¿ I said I'm not scared of anything. Oh, I thought I saw fear in those bulging eyes of yours. No, you didn't, I had an eye disease and they stayed this way, there's no cure, it's called bulging eyes. Cross my heart I could have sworn you were terrified. Don't be an idiot! You don't even know me! Oh, I don't¿ Who in this town hasn't heard of the Whore¿ That big-bellied bitch was pissing me off. Oh really, has your man already come to see me¿ Of course not, he's got good taste! This time it was me who couldn't hold my laughter in: Good taste¿ That's not what it looks like from where I'm sitting. What's your name, or is it really just Whore¿ I didn't know whores could get pregnant, she said, smiling and twisting her face in a grimace. I stood up and went to sit farther down the bench, the person to my left was sleeping with her mouth open but at least she was quiet. I was anxious, that place bugged me, all those women, all those bellies, all those beings about to be annihilated... I saw a slender woman leave the operating room carrying a big, rosy-cheeked baby in her arms, and I remembered that women didn't just go there to get abortions, they also went there to birth their children. Then I started to realize why Big Belly was upset, she didn't like that I was reckless, I'd heard her calling me murderer as I stood up. The midwife followed the slender woman out of the room, her smock covered in blood, and that was the first time I saw her, she looked scary, and I thought it must be terrible to be born face to face with that. She was short and curvy and, in a certain way, after I got a better look at her, I realized her ugliness was more funny than scary. Her face was stunted like some tiny God who had failed at getting revenge. Really, she looked exactly like an old fetus. She motioned with her tiny hands, indicating it was my turn. I took a little while getting up and she shouted. I wasn't in a hurry to walk over, I wasn't sure she'd pointed to me since there were other women who had gotten there well before me. I'm pointing at you, muchacha, the others still need to simmer a while longer, I can tell by the size of the feet. You scared, muchacha¿ Don't worry, no one's ever come out of here dead, except the ones with death in their eyes, she said, and laughed like a crazy gazelle. That's when I noticed she had huge gums and tiny teeth, that's what gave her that comical look. I stopped looking at her, it was all too strange and it was making my nausea worse. I got closer to her and asked her to get on with it, I'd already been waiting too long, I was tired and the more time that passed the more fused that thing became with my flesh. She looked at me for a long time and I tried to guess what was happening in that rat brain of hers, but all I could see was a dense fog. I couldn't tell if she was scolding me for my attitude or if she found it funny that I was in a hurry. For a minute I thought about explaining what was happening, however, thanks to that minuscule being I felt tremendously lazy and would have preferred to high tail it out of there, but I had no choice, I'd already tried everything, she was my only hope, even if she looked like she'd just left the loony bin. I didn't like the idea of placing my life in the hands of a little woman like that. And it seemed like she knew I didn't trust her at all. Relax, muchacha, she said, chortling and giving my thigh a quick slap, then, she returned her hand and patted my legs more forcefully the second time: nice, strong legs, eh, muchacha¿ If you wanted you could give birth in a squatting position, she chortled again, flashing her baby teeth. I stayed quiet, my body paralyzed, I was disgusted by her hands lapping at my legs, I don't know if she did it on purpose but she even grazed my clitoris. She didn't stop, she was still observing me, scrutinizing me, she had shrewd eyes, and she didn't realize it but she was searching for an object in an empty box. She could look as long as she wanted, she wasn't going to find anything, nothing at all. Outside, the women were scared of her, they said she could see the future and the past. Her intuition wasn't going to work on me, she wasn't going to find anything rotten inside me and I'd already been soulless a long time. She smelled like rue leaves and cilantro. It smelled pretty good, like freshly harvested herbs. Smelling it brought me a little relief and I thought maybe she wasn't that crazy. Or at the very least she was a lunatic that smelled like herbs. That piqued my interest somewhat because the only person in the region I knew who could grow herbs was my mother. But what did that matter, really¿ What mattered was that she get that kid out my stomach, the nausea was returning and I didn't want to go through it all again. If she didn't stop talking I might puke on her. I shouted, she tried to calm me down: don't worry, muchacha, in two minutes you'll be free, it won't even be two days before you're back on the dick again, then she stopped talking and again with the belly laugh. She brushed my face with her tiny hand. What's this, muchacha¿ You've got a water bubble in that face of yours, you better be careful, they say smallpox is back on your side of town. Don't mess around with that disease! Don't be stupid, it's just a wart that healed wrong, now can you stop talking and get this thing out of my stomach! Calm down, girl, I'll get it out! That's what it is then, I believe you, muchacha, if you say it's a wart, it's a wart, she laughed and stuck her hands between my legs, brushing my labia. I wanted to scream and swear, but then a pleasant little tingle crawled up my spine. She removed her hand unceremoniously, I don't know if she knew what she was doing, was I really that dizzy¿ I walked a little faster to get a safe distance away. But it wasn't long before she reached me again and said I shouldn't run off like that, it was rude to leave a woman empty-handed, then she laughed again and pinched my tit. It made me horny, even though I was nauseous. A mosquito was flying around her eye. She didn't care, she was playing it off or was already used to it. The insect started getting on my nerves, even though it wasn't my face it was circling. I followed the mosquito out of the corner of my eye, it only took a few moments before it tried to invade my line of sight, I swatted at it, it didn't try to follow me, it gave up quickly and my vision was clear again. I looked behind her ear expecting to find some explanation, but I couldn't see anything except a vague point and a large, infected pimple. I felt a little sick, imagining the pimple bursting at any moment. I couldn't get the image out of my head, I wanted to pop it right there and free myself from the presence of its purulent liquid. Yellowed wax made her deaf. She didn't seem to care, she didn't seem to care about anything! Nothing affected the peace of that amputated being. I don't know how some people live so removed from everything. I hate people like that. Despite being a small woman, she had ample tits, they weren't too hard or too soft, they were almost the perfect consistency. I could have shoved my hands between them and fallen asleep. She had a pack of cigarettes stuffed in her cleavage. Women like to hold their secrets close to the chest. I don't know why but I got an uncontrollable urge to pluck a cigarette from in there. I didn't understand it, but it was like that area of her body had me hypnotized. I couldn't stop thinking what it would be like to slurp a cigarette from that harvest, but I didn't pursue it. I'd smoked a few times, but only very casually—I'd smoke to ward off hunger, I'd smoke to please a client, I'd smoke after sex because some men liked to smoke after coming and I'd join them, but I never smoked because I craved it. Even before the war I'd never bought a pack of cigarettes, I'll admit I've been given many packs and I've taken a drag because I hate to waste, but I never spent money on it. But now, for the first time in my life, I felt the urgent need to take a pull, but not just any pull, not from just any pack, and not just any cigarette, it had to be that one, and more than that, it had to be damp with the sweat from her cleavage, my tongue dragging along her tits, suddenly my mouth was sopping wet imagining her hard tits. I snapped out of it, what a dark thought, that thing in my belly must be making me crazy. The rift wouldn't close, again I imagined my tongue drooling on her breasts and reaching for the cigarette. I imagined her offering me a drag at some point and, playing shy, I'd refuse. No thank you I'd say, I don't smoke. She'd insist, I'd refuse again, I would only accept on the third offer, after which I'd plunge my mouth into her cleavage and grab the cigarette between my teeth, then I'd drag my tongue across every centimeter of her chest, I'd alternate between the left and the right and then, after five minutes of salivating, she'd beg me to stroke and bite them. Just to spite her I wouldn't bite, I'd spend another five minutes licking and only then would I bite till she bled. Hey, muchacha, wake up, wake up, muchacha, she chortled, we're almost to the operating room, I hope you're ready, she said as she brazenly pinched my ass. I thought about cussing her out but my voice was stuck and for some reason I was a little wet, I could have touched myself right then and there and I'd have come in no time. A pig was strung up by its legs in the back of the room, its belly was open and blood was streaming into a bucket. Dark blood like the night. I thought the animal was a bad omen, something bad was happening, the rotted mouth behind the kisses. A daze almost knocked me over, but Flamenca grabbed me in time. I see you haven't been eating, muchacha, you won't be able to take it if you haven't. She was like a mosquito buzzing in my ear, but I didn't waste my time asking her to shut up, it was pointless, she wouldn't listen and she'd let out another chortle that would show off her gigantic gums. The bile and vomit rose to my mouth again. I controlled myself, I swallowed hard, tried not to breathe so I wouldn't smell that horrible blood smell. With each moment that passed I trusted this woman less. She had a sarcastic smile, like she was enjoying my suffering. I got the impression she could have finished the procedure by now, but that she was following a ritual where the wait was the main event. I could have already been free, on my own two feet, I could have been far from there, from that unsettling presence.

Without my permission my eyes returned to the hanging animal, it was screaming, it was still alive, the gash hadn't killed it. She wasn't lying, that animal really was alive. I was taken aback by the beast's strength, and ashamed of my own weakness. Don't tell me you're scared, muchacha¿ Don't be afraid my little muchacha, I'm not going to do anything to that animal, after I opened her up I realized she's pregnant, I'm just going to take a little blood for the sausage and then I'll stitch her back up, she'll be as good as new, you'll see. I don't like to see animals suffer, I'd kill her right away but I figured it's more lucrative to take advantage of a litter on the way. And I had a nasty craving for chouriço, so what could I do¿ I'd already cut into her, a little blood won't kill an animal that big. She had a strange accent, Spanish, or some dialect I'd never heard. She'd already been speaking into my ear for so long I was starting to understand her strange tongue. She kept talking for another fifteen minutes, explaining about animals, the proper way to kill them, about hanging them by their feet, how to cut them open and blah blah blah. I didn't understand a word, I was absorbed in my own problems, plus her accent bothered me. I saw her flapping her lips and waving her hands around like I knew what she was saying, but I thought it better not to pay attention to peanuts. She went on boasting, saying a good cook knows more about bones and joints than a doctor. I didn't object, what did I care about doctors or butchers¿ There was only one doctor left in town and the poor guy was about as thick as two short planks. What I really wanted was for her to stop chit-chatting and do something about this strange being that had invaded me and was taking up all my space. My waist had grown thirty centimeters in the past two weeks, no question I was pregnant with a monster, and if I wasn't careful it would swallow me whole before I managed to get it out. After an interminable wait she seemed to have decided to do her job. Take off your panties, that's right, the faster you do that the faster we can start and the faster we can finish, and she chortled. She had forgotten I'd been waiting for hours already. Now pull up that little skirt, if you want you can take all your clothes off, she said and pinched by breast again. Lay down on the table, yes, now relax, if you don't relax I can't do my job, don't worry, you're going to like what I do. Before I lay down, she removed a chunk of placenta she'd probably forgotten from the last abortion. *Let's go, muchacha, open those legs wide.* Así no, wider, fling 'em open, picture su cock mucho open. I know you're used to it, little girl, I can see it in your eyes, she said, chortling and rubbing my breast. I thought about swatting her filthy hands away, but instead I brought her closer, stuffed my fingers inside her underwear and told her to suck me 'til I came. She moved her soaking tongue fast and expertly over my nipples. She kept laughing while she licked me. I let out a satisfied groan. She wiped the drool that was running down her chin with the back of her hand and chortled. It would have annoyed me but my body was soft with pleasure. Then she got to work. She grabbed some sort of pipe, told me to relax again, this was a common procedure, you gotta poke the little guy, if you don't he won't come out. She pushed my labia aside, I felt a tingle, they were still sensitive. First, she used two fingers to loosen my pussy, which made me want to come again, then she very calmly inserted the pipe in my vagina. It was long and thick, and made of plastic or something like it. She didn't realize my cries weren't from pain. After a few moments, the thing started sucking at my belly with incredible force. I started feeling more confident, pretty soon it would all be handled, the whole ordeal would be behind me. I looked at her, she seemed apprehensive and the wrinkles on her face were growing. I couldn't figure out why she looked terrified, I wasn't feeling anything strange, if anything I was feeling relieved to get rid of that horrendous belly. Muchacha, I don't want to scare you, but I have to say something. Spit it out, lady, what's up, nothing seems off to me. Muchacha, don't mess around, don't talk about what you don't know, something very strange is happening here. Have you given birth before¿ Of course not! Have you ever terminated other muchachos, pequeña. Of course I have! And everything went fine, muchacha¿ Yes, yes, it was fine. Do you know who the father of this child is, muchacha¿ How would I know that¿ You think a whore has time to fall in love¿ I didn't mean that, muchacha, calm down, let's see what we can do, maybe there's a way. What's happening, what's with all this damn talking, where'd you throw the fetus, did you get it out already¿ That's the problem, muchacha, the boy won't come out, he's resisting the suction, I don't know what to do next, I've never seen this before. It's very strange, muchacha! I've never heard of anything like it. Normally they come out with one suck. I can see through this hole that your child who isn't even a child yet is all coiled up in there. It looks like a cornered cat. He won't come out. I'm going to try throwing a little hot water on it, muchacha, it'll hurt a little but maybe he'll get scared and decide to come out. I screamed in terror, my uterus was burning inside but no, the pest wouldn't budge. She kept up the suction for hours and hours. I spent a week with that pipe between my legs and nothing. My thighs were purple and my vagina oozed a dark and stinky mucus. I've never seen anything like it. Now he's clutching your fallopian tubes, he's behind your floating ribs. Are you alright, Muchacha¿ What a stupid question! Of course I'm not alright, I have a pipe between my legs and my body is covered in wounds, how could I be alright¿ Calm down, Muchacha, the little thing isn't screwed in there, it has to come out at some point, it has to! While he's still in there, take this Cuban cigar, it'll do you good. Will the cigar help, will it get this thing out of me??? No. But when there's nothing else to do, the best thing is to smoke a Cuban. And that's how I got addicted to Cuban cigars, boxes and boxes up in smoke. I've tried everything to quit, even the ritual of boiling the butts and drinking it on an empty stomach. I puked for three weeks straight but went back to smoking the minute I wasn't nauseous. The little shit wanted to stay in there, there was no way around it. After seven months, I called Flamenca to help me deliver. I didn't even need her, the kid slid out like a chunk of cooked okra, he was so used to the world that he didn't even cry, not even a meow, quite the opposite, in fact, he flashed a beautiful and toothless smile. He had wonderful gums. I begged Flamenca to move in with us, I didn't know what to do with something so small and ugly. He was soft, gelatinous, and ruminated all day long. It seemed likely one of us would end up dead if I was forced to be locked up with that strange creature all day. Flamenca listed around twenty reasons why she shouldn't stay, said everything in her life was planned and this wasn't part of it, she wouldn't be happy living under someone else's roof and under their rules, she also said even though she loved the idea of fucking me again she couldn't accept my proposal, it was almost indecent. She liked me, but sleeping in the same bed she wouldn't accept, no, no, no way, no one could make her change her mind. So I explained that it didn't have anything to do with sex or love, I didn't care if she wanted to sleep with me again or not, and fucking wasn't the issue, I wasn't lacking in that department, the issue was that weird creature, I needed help and she was the only person I knew around there, I wouldn't be her boss and the house would be hers too, I didn't care about anything, she could make any changes she wanted, I didn't care as long as she stayed and shared her breast with the kid, if not he'd starve to death, he hadn't eaten and I wasn't going to let that freak ruin my tits. Flamenca looked at me with cunning eyes, one minute she'd glance at me, the next she'd glance at the boy, then she said: I won't stay, there's no way, you think I'm dumb¿ She started talking like a rattle, told me of various tragedies she'd avoided all because she knew when to say no, and she talked and talked so much I stopped listening, her accent rolled around between my ears and her hands wove landscapes I'd never visited. And that's that, Muchacha, you're heard me right, I won't stop being a midwife just so I can park myself in this hole, it's decided. Those women you saw in the hallway need me, what were you thinking¿ That I'm useless, a nobody¿ Know this, Muchacha, lots and lots of people have made me better offers. Take your own tits out and feed the kid, he'll like it, if I remember he's got good taste, Muchacha, she said, laughing and pinching my butt. I didn't find it funny, I wasn't in the mood for jokes, if she didn't want to stay she didn't need to keep rubbing her filthy hands on my ass. My patience was hanging by a thread, I thought about cussing her out, kicking her out, dragging her across the ground until she said yes. But I didn't need to, I got distracted and looked away for a moment, and when I looked back, there was Flamenca, sitting and laughing with her tits dangling in the boy's mouth. I smiled wickedly and said: so you're staying¿ No, no, Muchacha, it's not like that, I'm just giving him a little of what he wants, he looked at my chest so nasty I felt bad denying him, poor thing. He's ugly but he's human, she laughed, showing off her giant pink gums. Flamenca did everything she could not to stay, erected all kinds of barriers, established a thousand boundaries, made me promise hundreds of things, but in the end, I think she stayed because she took a liking to the blind dependence that child had on her tits. She said she'd be leaving soon, that I shouldn't get used to it, she liked muchachos, so she'd help out, but soon she started saying she couldn't sleep if I didn't eat her out. I found that request completely unreasonable and I don't know why I agreed to it, and I have even less of an idea why I spent every night eating her pussy. Flamenca stayed, and quickly acclimated to her new life, her new chores. For a long time she forgot she was a midwife, she became strangely disconnected from her past. She only went back to her old house to grab the litter of piglets. Like I said, muchacha, I don't like to waste, even more so in these troubled times, there's no greater sin than wasting food. A day later she came back surrounded by hairy white pigs. Moving was good for her, it gave her a sudden strength. She didn't even seem like the same frail woman, her body had taken on a certain vigor and her face a different shade of red. She ran around all day talking to herself in an incomprehensible dialect, I tried to understand her a few times but gave up quick. She didn't care, she just wanted to gab, even if no one was listening. A few times I entertained the thought that she didn't want anyone to understand her, because that way she could say whatever mumbo jumbo came to mind. The days passed and I figured I'd never be the same. She would get up early and as soon as the boy started crying, she'd give him her teat, and he'd plunge his hands into her cleavage voraciously, sucking away like a pervert. I'd just stand there watching, I never understood breastfeeding as a gesture of love, it seemed more like an act of desperation, of solitude. The apple never falls far from the tree. I hardly had any contact with my son, he was glued to Flamenca. Her tits were now large and firm like two papayas. The kid wasn't a baby anymore and still he wouldn't leave the teat. Flamenca would chortle and say leave him alone, he's got good taste. I didn't fuss over them, they seemed to understand each other. They played hide-and-seek and tag all day. I have to admit that having Flamenca and that tiny creature around changed me eventually, at first I was hard like a rock, then I became more like hot magma. I ended up getting used to the peaceful life, waking up and having another pair of eyes staring at me. I spent a long time trying to figure out if it was good or bad. I never managed to decide, but I know I liked waking up and smelling the potatoes boiling in the kitchen and hearing the corn cracking on the fire. I also got used to the smell of the herbs behind Flamenca's ear. And the boy's cries grew thinner with each passing year. I woke up a little late one day and noticed he'd gotten old, he was already a man. His facial hair reached from one side of his face to the other, a curtain hiding his intentions, and his ear, which before was soft and smooth, now sported small, dark, curly hairs. The ridge of his nose had become raised and his forehead gathered the way old men's do. His tongue thickened the sounds of his words and his words had become scarce-sputum. Although still young, he was the image of decay and decay made me sick. I stayed the same, even if inside I had become a softer, more moldable dough. The boy hardly spoke to me, and when he wanted to ask me something he'd whisper it low in Flamenca's ear for her to pass along. He didn't call me mom and the few times he had the courage to address me directly, he called me senhora. Me, the whore, now a reputable senhora in that strange boy's eyes. One of his eyes was smaller than the other and his left eye was always shaking like a castaway's. This world wasn't made for him, and I quickly realized that he wasn't going to stick around for the long haul, that soon he'd pack his bags and be on his way, in search of less granulated lands. But his departure occurred under circumstances I could never have imagined. The boy had barely reached fifteen when he announced he was getting married. His eagerness shocked me, because he'd never heard anyone in that country allude to such an institution. Weddings were killed off in the war. I would never have spoken of something so dark, I might not have loved him as much as other moms love their offspring, but I didn't wish him ill, and I would never have preached the wonders of married life, I wouldn't have been capable of throwing him down a hole so deep. What a crazy idea, kid! How do you know what marriage is¿ Who taught you something so absurd¿ Nothing so despicable could have ever come from my mouth! Have you ever been stung by a scorpion¿ Then you better shut up! Have you been hanging out with a foreigner¿ Did someone new show up in town¿ I haven't seen any strangers around! Who put these ideas in your head¿ What about the bride¿ Do you have any idea what a bride is¿ Veil, bouquet, the whole shitty kit-and-kaboodle¿ You've never even known a woman's body, kid. Have you ever stuck your hand up a pussy¿ Have you ever sucked on a woman's tits¿ Forget it, this craziness won't get you anything but heartbreak! Men are easily suffocated by women's false sweetness. But, Mom, I want to! I've never spoken to you, Mom, there's a labyrinth between my mouth and your ears, but today desire has shaped that labyrinth and I'm begging you to listen to me. I've never asked you for anything and I'm not asking now, I just wanted you to know, I didn't want to leave without making some noise, without letting the back door slam. I like how this house smells, the gaps, the slats, the holes in the ground, the lizards that live in the walls; I know every inch of this ruin, this disgrace, but that doesn't stop me from wanting to stay, to stretch my legs out on top of that crate over there. I want to crouch down and crack every one of my toes. And even for you, who has never shown me an ounce of affection, even for you I feel a certain tenderness. Even for the dogs I devour. But I've grown up, Mom, you can't crush me anymore or try to rip me from your uterus. Your uterus stinks now and I don't need your placenta for sustenance. The egg presupposes the bird's torture, the agony of flight. Sooner or later, you knew this day would come. You pretended because you got used to the company, no one has figured out how to be happy alone yet, that's why even God created the Devil from his phlegm. Don't act stupid, kid! You're talking like an old man! No, Mom, I'm talking like someone who knows what love is. Love expands the physical body, and I feel obese. Besides, I'm not a boy anymore, look at my face, look at the size of my pants, things have changed around here, you've just been too busy jumping from bed to bed... Show me some respect, boy! You didn't get that audacity from me! I'm the only reason you're here, thanks to my big belly, the cord tied to my belly button. I'm sorry, Mom, but if I'm here it's thanks to Flamenca, not you, she was the one who gave me the nipple my entire life. If it were just you, I'd have starved to death. If it had been up to you, Mom, that pipe would have sucked me out till I disappeared. I'd be buried in the cemetery of the unborn. I find it funny to call this piddly shit a life, stop being so dramatic, kid,

I was the one who asked Flamenca to come live here. Speaking of Flamenca, where is she¿ She's around here somewhere, I'll call her over, she needs to be part of this conversation, maybe even more than you could imagine. What you don't know about women is a lot. Have you ever been bit by a cobra¿ Of course not, Mom! So you don't know the fury of a woman's body. To get married you have to have slept with the bride. Men get married when they have a bride, where is your bride? I have a bride, Mom. You have a bride? That's a laugh! I wasn't expecting to hear so much bullshit come out of your mouth, you ungrateful little boy! And where is she, can you tell me that? I've never seen the shadow of a skirt around here. You must be confusing men with women. Kid, you don't know what's waiting for you out there! You don't want to walk out there with silly ideas about finding a wife, no one who's left this town has ever come back, either there's something incredible on the other side and no one's ever bothered to send word or there ain't shit. And I suspect there's nothing, just a white river, a very white river. You don't want to go wandering off after nothing, it's sad to leave with empty hands and your hunchback sweaty from solitude. But I already have a bride, Mom, I'm not going searching for one, she's right here with me. What do you mean, boy¿ Am I the one that's crazy¿ There's no woman here or am I going blind¿ Show me this bride of yours. The boy placed his hands on Flamenca's shoulders, then slid them down her back, and when he reached her waist, he stopped. I couldn't believe what I was seeing, there had to be some mistake, he was trying to say one thing but, accustomed as he was to silence, he was tripping over his words. I looked firmly at Flamenca, waiting for an explanation or something like one. Flamenca is my bride. See, Mom, I'm not crazy. I can see you don't know anything about marriage, maybe you're not crazy, but you're definitely naive! People who are naive are even more dangerous than idiots! Flamenca is more your mom than your bride. Up until recently you were breastfeeding like a weaning calf, you'd suck on one and palm the other. The two of you spent all day running around playing tag, hide-and-seek, mãe da rua, amarelinha, and who the fuck knows what else. I don't care what you think, we're leaving so we can be together. We'll be one body, one flesh. Then later, we'll multiply. I don't want to die before seeing my fruits plummeting onto the earth. My testicles are swollen, its urgent, life's instinct is pulsing inside me. As he spoke, he squeezed his balls with his fingers and gave me a look of insufferable insolence. I've never had patience for young peoples' pretension. Flamenca, tell him this is crazy, the thoughts of a foolish boy, a boy with chickenshit for brains. Please, take this weight off my shoulders, help me like you always have. But we're in love. In love? In love¿ My head felt like a pressure cooker, I couldn't believe the insanity I was being forced to listen to, I was being pelted from all angles. Flamenca, don't tell me you believe this lie too. You're not some naive little girl who would have a stake in something like this! A month ago you were still sneaking into my room, murmuring in my ear, licking my body, offering up your tits, stuffing your fingers between my legs and now you want to get married¿ Where'd you get that idea from, have you gone crazy¿ What do you really want¿ Wasn't it you who was always saying you wanted to treat the kid right and now here you come with this cock and bull story¿ Don't let me down, Flamenca! You're lying, there's no way you're in love, I won't believe it! I can still feel your spit dripping off my clit. Did you forget where you used to be, where you came from¿ Did you forget what you're into¿ Did you forget what you like, you aren't used to sucking dick! I'd never allow something like this, you can't be serious! Your body's never known a man's body, you don't know what they require, you wouldn't know what to do with one, you have no idea how to work a dick, your body was made for slathering up women. Forget all this, I'm begging you! Your pussy is too clapped out to make a curve, it's all grooves, cysts, tight and dark folds. Don't take the boy down that labyrinth. You've spent too much time messing around with your own body, you don't want to give him a poison fruit. You know this is ridiculous, at some point he'll meet other women—real women, not this five-and-dime version—and he'll realize how much he hates you, how bad you duped him, he'll look in your eyes and see those cataracts plummet, and when he sees a beautiful woman, he'll blame you for being old. You are old, you better believe it! You got old, I saw it, I watched your body's rapid decline. Think about it, Flamenca, passion is for the young, you don't have any right to it anymore. Our time's been up for a long while, get used to it and come lie with me, first I'll lick your whole body, then I'll offer you mine, come on, eat me out like you used to, I miss your tongue, forget all this, even just thinking about it gets me wet.

Don't be stupid, Anúncia, don't try to trick me with your sieve body, full of pitfalls, I want to get to know cocks now, I know I wasn't interested before but now I am. Don't make me feel bad for you! I decided I can't die without knowing love and, contrary to what you think, love does belong to the old, to settled souls, stretch marks help ground young people's feet on the muddy earth, passion looks good at any age and I'd say the old are more prone to passion, rusty bells chime just as loud as new ones. Simulacra are eternally young, regardless of the craziness of time. Let me live, Anúncia, you can't stop me, and you can't convince your son, he's already been hooked. You are well aware, Flamenca, that he's an idiot. He's the only one who can't see there's no bait on that rusty hook. I could tell my words were useless, as insignificant as all the familial discourse that came before mine. All men, all of them, have tried to give some boundless importance to words, make them more potent than action, but the truth is that instinct and desire rein supreme. At times like that, words are little more than inaudible grunts. I was a declining whore, and offering my body wasn't going to get me anywhere, who would want a corrupted flower¿ Who but my own litter would have fallen into so dirty a trap¿ I didn't have anything else to offer, a tremendous fatigue was corroding my bones, I was old. I really had gotten old, who would have thought! I, who always thought whores were immune to time. A nostalgia dominated my tongue, it slumbered in my mouth, and for some reason I remembered the fish carcasses along the river. I remembered when the philosopher lay next to me and played with my breasts while he tried to formulate his ideas. A philosopher who doesn't believe in ideas isn't a philosopher, he's a cynic. What's the point of so many ideas¿ He had certainly also gotten old, he, who spent his whole life trying to explain the origin of knowledge, seeking purity where there was only mud. I looked at my son again and realized how much he looked like his father, despite his brutality. I shook my head and saw they were still frozen in front of me. For a second I was scared they'd heard my thoughts, but no, they hadn't heard anything, they weren't worried about me. I didn't say anything else, I extended my hands and waited for them to extend theirs. I wanted to say good luck, but the sound didn't come out, it got lost halfway through. They took a long time to notice my offer, and by the time they held out their arms I'd already lowered mine. I looked in Flamenca's eyes, a botfly was perched on her eyelid. I waved my hand but it didn't move. And I had no idea she had skin that moved over her eyes! I was stunned! I always thought she was a woman without eyelids, a woman who was attentive like a fish. I was wrong! I tried to tell her but it was useless, neither of the two could see the insect. I swatted my hand to scare it. Nothing. I ran into them again three years later, the fly was dead by then and her eyes stank like horse shit—fresh horse shit. I motioned for them come in. I pointed to the door, even though I knew they knew the way. I sighed and said that by some miracle the white fig had fruited. I didn't really know what to say, I didn't know what they wanted to hear. They looked at me and their expressions remained as changeless as if not a single comma had slipped past my mouth. I took a deep breath and tried again, asked if they had found anything on the other side, asked them to tell me about it. They traded a look, I don't know if it was conspiratorial, but they remained silent. I walked ahead of them and opened the door, it was obviously an invitation, it might as well have been a supplication. They refused, asked only for a little water and dry bread, they had to continue on their journey, it took a lot of walking to reach the promised land. I asked where they were headed, I asked about kids and they went quiet and bowed their heads like they were confessing to a crime they hadn't yet committed. I also went quiet, I could tell they were no longer the same, our ties had come undone, I almost couldn't believe that man had come out of me, I almost couldn't believe that woman had licked my body. He opened his mouth like he was making a great sacrifice. We're a nomadic people, what use is there in knowing where we're going. I thought I was used to being abandoned. I don't know, something was bothering me, I ran my hand along my body and felt grooves. I missed Flamenca's accent echoing through the house, I missed her inane laughter. They came back every once in a while and asked for water; their eyes stank increasingly worse, and grew deeper. What kind of sickness was that¿ Her lashes, which used to be full, were gone, leaving two naked eyes in her face. Her mouth was twisted, and her thick tongue had formed a white crust. Even though she'd stopped smoking, I could see the smoke pluming from between her dingy fingers. They walked in circles. Their feet cracked then grew husks, their steps became ruminant. One day they had a dog they'd stuffed into a collar with them. I couldn't tell if they were walking the dog or if it was guiding them. On the next visit the collar contained a skinny black bull, maybe they were waiting on it to fatten up before they took it to slaughter. I could see Flamenca crouching down from far off, ripping out some greens and bringing them to the beast's mouth. In Flamenca's good eye a pale blue was growing. I knew they'd always come back, sooner or later. The umbilical cord was still buried in the yard. Things are born, die, then regrow at any moment. I never paid much attention to those kinds of things, but Flamenca insisted, said if I threw the cord away the boy would get lost out there. She'd seen it lots of times, children out in God knows where becoming men, just because the parents refused to bury the umbilical cord. Go right ahead, Flamenca, with your silly superstitions, turns out you've got confused-thick-coagulated blood in your nostrils. Don't start thinking I'm worried about this kid's future, he only got born 'cause he's headstrong, I didn't ask for any of it, I opened my legs and he fell out, like a pear falls, or a mango. I've met lots of women who gave their lives for their kids and then, little by little, they dried right up. It's ugly to dry up like that, gently, like a rotten fruit forgotten on the stem. First, the kids would sell the curtains, the furniture, mortgage the house, then, finally, sell off their mothers for a few miserable coins. Ingratitude is a fungus, a thrombosis that cuts you down at the legs. Most things weren't a choice, they were forced destiny. Now, I choose when I can. Up until now I've stayed away from things that could amputate me, I won't start treating myself to them now. If you want to, do it, and if you don't, roll that thing up in a plastic bag 'cause it's almost garbage day. I said it with conviction even though the garbage had been piling up outside the door for years, no man came by to collect our scraps in town, everyone dealt with their own shit. Mine was massive. An entire sewer with each shit. Don't say that, senhora, you don't understand things, concrete can be molded before it gets hard. What goes around comes around. Look at me, look how I've changed over the years. Flamenca, you got old, and you've only gotten dumber. Let me make something clear, I'm not an affectionate woman, I'm a survivor. Instinct taught me to live alone and alone is how I know to live. I cook in a pan for one. You two showed up and ruined everything. Now I hear zoom zoom zoom all day long. A jump rope hitting the ground every once in a while. Go on, Flamenca, get off my back. Senhora, past the two rose bushes outside there's a white fig. I'll go out early tomorrow and bury the boy's umbilical cord there. The dirt likes to be tilled. Those who don't set down roots lead feeble lives, and any bullet can pull the soul out the carcass. I don't care if you don't want to look out for him, I'll do it. I've done lots of stupid things in this world—I'm a woman no bird has ever had a perch near. I've wrung a chicken's neck just for fun then slurped the fresh blood out. Purely for malice. I've already killed lots of kiddos but I don't think that matters now. Actions leave deep lines behind, like an anus blooming outward, ruined by the years. I don't regret it, I did what they ordered me to do. Sad that pity is something I've never known. My deaths were of another kind. A mixture of many hands and little faith. The war racked up its fair share of numbers too. That's the thing, my deaths couldn't be computed, they hadn't been born yet. I forgive myself for having unraveled many fetuses. Pulled affectionately at a string and watched the whole thorax come apart in my hands. This boy is different, he withstood weeks and weeks of suction. If he's not a saint, he's the devil himself. And in either case I'm on his side. Do what you want, just don't harass me, I need a good night's sleep. That kid hollers all night. Either I'm wrong or your milk is garbage. If I had the patience, I'd feed the waif myself. Don't complain so much, senhora, his eyes are still getting used to this darkness. I've seen lots of men who only got used to it well past their seventies. That won't be the case with him. He came out of a liquid reality and needs to learn to live with the concreteness of things. You've changed, Flamenca, you're starting to scare me with all this talk, what's going on¿ Did you get motherly all the sudden¿ You've been getting on my nerves, you're hardly even good in the sack anymore, always drooling over the kid, he'll grow up soon and you'll see, you'll be all alone and I won't be your shoulder to cry on. She got quiet, when she didn't want to answer me she pretended she couldn't hear me or that she needed to check the stove or save the boy from some potential accident. Flamenca wore me out with her stories of a distant town. A bad woman who got it in her head that her mission was to take care of my son. We'll see where that gets her. In the end, I was wrong, my son didn't leave her, they both left me, I birthed them both and I became diasporic. Flamenca had never known a dick, I birthed her.

When I met her she was just a clumsy puckered fetus, all she knew was vaginas <the negative>, all she knew was how to please women, cloning her fingers and transforming them into an erect and articulating cock. What did I get out of that¿ Nothing, now that he's been born of my loins he eats his own brother, the brother that hid behind my ribs so as not to be banished. From mother and son, they became lovers. I couldn't warn my son of the dangers of women. The third time he appeared he had a cut on his back at the height of his last vertebra. I didn't ask what happened. I knew, he was becoming a man, a great man. I also didn't have the chance to warn Flamenca about men. Before him, she'd only loved women. She only knew the secrets and tricks of females. She didn't know the malice of men, their desire to shove their cocks in our guts. Her eye shrank at the rate the fly decomposed. Horses trotted on his spine and shat on her face. I wanted to cry, but I wasn't an affectionate woman. I can't say their departure affected me, I hardly knew them before they left. Absence is a white cockroach. They'd go months without appearing. One night I looked through the crack, not that I was waiting for them, but it was hot and I couldn't breathe. I saw a figure behind the small tree, but I couldn't quite make it out, I thought maybe it was Flamenca, but I wasn't sure. I decided to go to the other crack, which was bigger, and when I got there I saw a brown package in the yard. I didn't know whether to stay kneeling on the floor or get up and see what the package was. Curiosity is one of humanity's greatest ills, I took my knee out of the dust and clapped my hands to startle the evil eye. I dragged myself to the door, opened the bolt, and went out. It must be something stupid, maybe a cow's eye or a horse tooth. Flamenca used to say that horse teeth scared evil spirits, maybe she wanted to do something nice for me. I opened the tiny package, blood eked through the paper and stained my hand. I tried to wipe it on my thigh, but the blot spread and I couldn't get it out. It was a fetus. Flamenca was nearby. I smelled the rotten stench of her eye sockets, I heard the sound of her vertebrae knocking against each other. I saw discharge tinting her clitoris. I took the package inside, grabbed a jar and threw the fetus in. Then I put it on top of the crate. The crate wobbled then returned to its customary silence. The darkness grew inside the prison. The plants grew and died during an uncountable interval. Or there never were any plants. I questioned whether I was still alive. The hallucinogens made me confused. I don't know what was worse, what was really happening or what I was hallucinating. In one of the dreams, I swallowed a shark and could breathe underwater. The sounds of the rats and the pigeons in the ceiling made me realize my life wasn't over. They figure my brain is already gangrenous. It was years of torture. But the mutilations didn't buy my silence. My clitoris still groans. Every day I masturbate to remember I'm still alive. I can still procreate. Like an animal. Crouching, I see the world breaking. A massive pile of shit. The fetus, although apparently dead, seemed animated in its jar, you still couldn't make out its facial features, or if there was a face there at all, but its eyes were alive like a plastic doll's eyes and a very confused shade of blue. They weren't mine, those eyes, and they weren't Flamenca's either, maybe it was blind, I had no way of knowing, but once or twice I saw a bubble in the liquid and an umbilical cord floating close to the jar's edge. That slender beast was so ugly, its wrinkled skin, it was hideous! And its nails grew so fast, they were huge like talons… I started to fear that strange animal I had trapped inside with me, that insect so similar to a man, was it some simian offspring¿ Why would Flamenca do this to me¿ She knew how disgusted I was by monkeys, I don't think she could have been that perverse after everything we'd been through together, we'd lived basically as husband and wife before it all went down… Well, I could never have imagined she'd fuck my son, my son who she helped birth and raise, my son who she breastfed. No, she wouldn't have been capable of that, she knew how much I hated monkeys. I don't know why, but I've never liked primates, they always seem like they're laughing at humanity's absurd condition, while at the same time they envy it. I don't trust monkeys even a little bit, they're traitors the same way tiny-dicked men are. Sometimes I wonder if it's not some kind of punishment, if I died and this is hell's veranda. I can see the bloody femur from here. With each passing day it grows closer to the crack. These visions have dogged me for years. When I was a kid, I liked to stare at woodcutting gouges. With time, I started touching men's and women's bodies and noticed that their skin also contained similar ruts. My thing was to move my fingers along and pretend I was reading a book in braille. I'd imagine that only the blind were happy. It wasn't the first time, it was normal to see pieces of body mirrored. I used to put a small mirror, one of those everyday orange ones you see on bathroom walls, in front of the crack. That way I didn't have to spend all my time watching on my knees, upset. I'd walk around the hole, doing what had to be done. There are lots of things to get done. You know better than me. Everyone knows, even if they're suicidal. When I couldn't take it anymore, I'd take the mirror off its nail, sprinkle some powder, and rail it. Cocaine gave me an agility and mental strength that few possess. Then I'd circle around for hours, I'd shout and answer my own echo. Then I'd put the mirror between my thighs and my hand between my thighs and the mirror. I used to pretend I was a crowd. All ghosts appear when solitude is raging beneath our nails. The fungi disappear. I've always been fond of dialogue. It tore up my tongue, it's true. I don't know many people who use their tongues when they talk. Eyelashes are more genuine and protect us from unclear conversations. Intervals traces silences. Conversations with tongues are infinite between parentheses. Boring and tiresome. During my exile I've learned to be succinct. I started to better understand things when my mouth was closed. Curdled milk in the jug. The silent botfly collapsing the flesh beneath the skin. The herb growing and mixing with the ivy. Ancient markings on the wall. Paint beneath other paint. Not the marrow, maybe it's still hiding, inside, in the guts of our bones. I'd blink unhurriedly and it remained there. No, it wasn't a mirage. It was real—sometimes we bump into reality. A sliver, a rock, a dagger. Obscene, almost an erection. Within a few minutes, the bones reminded me of Greek tragedies. I was never interested in theater, but I did see a certain meaning in catharsis. Living was an imitation of our ancestors' calamities. That was my grandmother's philosophy, wait around and you'll end up doing the same as that bitch mother of yours, and probably for less. That was all I saw from the hole I lived in. A massive bloody femur. Even as a child, I was fascinated by the abyss. I was mute, I didn't talk, if left alone I wouldn't eat. I'd tear off the clothes they insisted on dressing me in. I'd attack anyone who came near. At age five they put me in a collar like a bitch. Took to tossing a pot of leftover food in front of me and leaving. They didn't want to be accused of child abuse. Neighbors would come by and get incensed, men from neighboring towns would look and get incensed, strangers would cross oceans to see the wolf girl and get incensed. She's just retarded, that doesn't mean she deserves to be in a collar or treated like an animal. The president also looked and got incensed. Gave his ruling. Don't shove your snout in other people's kibble. Only we know the extent of our own evils. Then they all looked at each other less incensed and went back to their lives. They didn't hear anything more about the girl who fed on human anguish. Now she lived in a cubbyhole, and for some unknown reason I wasn't sad about it. She retained none of her previous exhibitionism. She'd take off her shirt and show that her muscles were becoming less animal, more human. She'd run her hand along her chest to reveal a hairless abdomen. She didn't like anything that suggested irrationality. She had restrained sex, swore in French to show she was civilized. She didn't like questions about her past. A real man is one without a shadow. Everything with a shadow drags other people's hell along with it. My skin doesn't carry the odorous mark of my ancestors. I was only that which you see before you. Why more? Are you not content with what you see? A well-trodden path is sadness. A cemetery is no place for the living. Self-portraits don't speak and skeletons don't tell stories, they're quiet because they're supreme. Mediocre are those who tell stories like strangers. I'm present time. Bodies often explode after death. And you know what the bang sounds like¿ It's like this, just a regular old finger snap. He liked to expose himself, like a butcher shop carcass. I don't know if it was before or after. Before I met him, I liked to observe people so I could draw them. The drawings grew increasingly abstract, took on their own style. Later I had a phenomenal idea: instead of drawing people, I'd try to guess what their genitalia looked like. I was amazingly good at it. A clairvoyance that wasn't good for anything except keeping me entertained. Every time I had the chance to check the veracity of my work, it was clear how good it was. But after him, things changed, it was like I'd lost my touch, he put a spell on me, I couldn't see the size of things clearly, objects became vague, and genitals... Well, I was no longer able to draw them effectively, the details escaped me, the spots, the color, the roughness, the scale, the exact number of hairs. My nose was crooked, maybe it got that way from all the beatings I took. I didn't breathe right, I suffocated at night. Lost sleep. I spent hours looking up and noting the paths of the stars. I couldn't understand it but sometimes the insomnia would go away and I'd fall asleep. The truth is my head had hurt for over a week. There were no medicines or teas that could help ease the pain and in a certain way I considered physical pain a way of communing with the sacred. That is definitely not a good defense for a crime. I don't want to justify anything, that's not my intention. To recount, with the objectivity of an insane person or a fiction writer, that's what I want. You could hear the bells chiming nearby, nearby inside me. Two cows walked around on my forehead. They chewed the cud, they cut my thoughts in half. The time between visits from Flamenca and my son grew longer from one visit to the next. I was almost getting used to living alone again, it never should have been any different. We look at a hen and forget she burst the egg, but she never forgets, she searches the whole yard, cracking-breaking into the same shell day after day. After my son and Flamenca left, lots of people started showing up in town, men, women, old people, children. The men that arrived were a strange breed, they didn't speak, didn't smile, didn't shout—they all lived together in absolute silence. But I knew something wasn't right. I saw a red mark on their faces, and it scared me, I remembered the great plagues of history, the incurable illnesses that preceded the last war. I kept my distance, but in a short time those silent men sought out my bed. And I wasn't able to fend them off. All their members were the same in size, color, curvature, rigidity. It was impossible to forget those identical cocks, and, I must confess, I've never come so hard. One day they all showed up together and I opened myself up to receive them. One afternoon I heard noises in the yard and I figured they were seeking me out again. I was squatting, it was a cloudy day, I was messing around with the roots, trying to wake them up, but it wasn't them, it was the Poet returning. I didn't expect him to come back but I'll admit I liked feeling distant from myself again, in that breed of multiplicity and horror that is another. He let out a grunt and I was able to recognize him. He was different, his clothes were tattered and his smell wafted for kilometers. I wanted to open my mouth to say something but he didn't allow it, he lowered down to match my size, placed his hand on my ass, touched my asshole, then put his fingers in my pussy, said he carried in him the hunger of all the men who had returned from war. I tried to push him away, his stench was overwhelming, it was almost impossible to handle, but instead I clenched my nostrils and powered through, his hands were determined and I was a solitary whore, a whore who appreciated a good dick, I got down on all fours right then and there and waited for him to finish what he'd started. I bounced, I bounced until it shot out hot and thick. You've really gone downhill since the last time we met. Yes, it's true, my dear, life has committed horrors against me, I can't even remember anymore. It's not easy to have the retina of a poet and the ugly and thick-skinned body of a billy goat. Have you ever slept rubbing a goat's dick¿ If you haven't you should try, they say they fuck better than any man or woman who ever set foot on this earth. You know, a lot has happened since the last time I saw you, I picked up a wife, a kid, these bizarre things people generally call a family, but an artist can't be content with tending the lawn. I got tired of it, left, spent months bumming around until I remembered you. You're one funny son of a bitch, you know that, who would remember a whore¿ Take it from me, my dear, whores and mothers you never forget. And what do you want from me¿ From you¿ Don't worry, my flower, I don't want anything, I made a decision some time ago. And what was that, Poet¿ I'm going to write a book. You've gotta be kidding, no one cares about books, did you forget there's no meaning in those anymore¿ And when was there¿ No one writes books because they're searching for meaning, they just write them, like an animal that eats and shits, like a woman who fucks, like a dog that eats shit. Thus... whatever floats your boat. I've already decided, I won't have a home or a family, on the road is where I'll be, and I'll write the greatest book ever written. I wanted to tell someone, that's all, that's why I came looking for you, I wanted someone to know. All right, now I know. Are you planning on staying the night¿ No, I can't stay, it's tempting, I love fucking you, but my journey has already begun, I'll be around, I'll find you when I need a lap to crawl into, if something goes wrong; I'll be hunting the word, that essential word that always escapes us, the sincerest part of speech. I'm bowing out of here, I'll only return when my book is done, and that's a promise. I didn't expect him to come back, I don't know many people capable of keeping a promise. He was crazy, I didn't argue, I let him think something existed to be said, knowing the most he'd manage would be narrative upchuck. For a long time, all we've needed has been grunts, but we've never needed words, all speech is an affront to instinct. Man dominated the grunt out of pure foolish necessity, by believing it was the form in which he wouldn't crawl on four legs like a reptile.

I lowered down and licked my thighs, used my saliva to clean my vulva, which still held a glob of cum. I heard yowling, prayers, and banging coming from the other side. I got up and squinted, I couldn't see anything, a thick dust covered the sky, and the sky was murky. I started thinking I was responsible for all that banging, for all those infinite prayers, for the clay angels, for the hollow saints projecting truths no one would follow. Liars, a big bunch of liars. They put on their best clothes, lined up in front of God then took a shit in the gutter right after. Huge hypocrites and me, lost, profane, and without a hymn to save me. God's saliva corrodes my face and the only thing I know to do is mourn, mourn for the men I beheaded after they fingered me, after they licked my clit. Tossed into a slot between the sky and the hot asphalt. A whore. Whores don't perform miracles. They just swallow spit and spunk. They lick their teeth clean for fear they'll reproduce. Alone in the mud I choose to dig around in the swamp, select the fattest crab, imprison it, watch it struggle impotent in the can's finitude, it realizes it's not eternal. Its little life was as cheap and ordinary as mine. I tended to walk backwards, too. Five reais and no leftovers, not even the undigested husk. A strange mirror of myself. The white powder disperses. A cathedral of obscenities. I fit my hands between its fingers, the love is singular, I see myself in love, crazy in love with this animal. Cacti are born—manure in the mangrove swamp. And I see myself as someone else. Almost a simulacrum of myself. Placebo. I want to untangle my fingers and be free again. Be able to see the revulsion an arthropod provokes again. I can't. I put my fingers down my throat but the bile doesn't rise. I'm a disgraced whore and freedom is just the name of a city park. I take the oysters off the bull, sprinkle a little salt on them and swallow. I feel better. The sun isn't beating down anymore and the clouds are plumping up. There was a wake before the downpour. It was him, even though he was bad as the devil, I knew that one day he'd die. Same as I knew that, despite my disaffection, I'd weep, make a quiet scandal, spend nights and nights awake searching for scarabs to protect him on his passage. One sunless morning, eyes swollen from crying, I saw a scarab preparing a small ball of excrement, I wanted to throw up but I hadn't eaten in weeks so there wasn't anything to get rid of, it put what appeared to be an egg in there, pushed it for a while and then started burying it. Before the insect noticed me, I pinched its colorful carapace with my thumb and pointer finger. I cleaned the rest of the excrement from its feet and put it in the corpse's mouth, who accepted it placidly. I looked out the window, or better, through the hole growing between two bricks. There's nothing else outside. I see the birds churning the earth and stealing the last of our seeds. The drive to live pushes towards rebeginning. Flamenca hasn't been around for a long time. I'd like to see her eyes again, the Ciranda of illusions spinning around in her open stomach. She has a war injury that never healed, you can see her whole digestive system at work. The doctor is always pushing me to lock Flamenca in the house so he can better understand how her body works. I can't. Bipartite Flamenca is like me, she's an embryonic split. No beginning or end, she multiplies suddenly, although like a leprotic animal she leaves a few fibrous pieces in her wake. The jar keeps growing. I see each of the being's limbs growing and differentiating—I still can't make out its sex, can't tell if what's growing in there is a penis or a vagina. No, it's not just what's inside the jar that grows larger and more animated. The jar itself is growing too, as if it were also an animal of flesh and bone, a tiny glass god. My breasts are large and heavy like two ripe melons, and they leak dark and bitter milk. I don't understand exactly what's happening, but I like to ponder the jar, it's like the birth of the sunset, hostile to ruin. And it seems my eyes animate the content and what encases it even more. The jar is like an artificial placenta, gelatinous and transparent. I've never been moved by birth, death has scared me a few times because a lifeless body looks like a rubber doll, like an empty box without an echo—a restless boy's crib—all the wrinkles smooth out and an entire life of suffering becomes a howl. Conversely, the emergence of Man makes him equal to animals, to quadrupeds, to arthropods. Looking through the glass each day, however, and seeing an organ emerge or perfect itself I get the impression that we're marvelous and singular beings, and our embryos aren't so similar to those of consumptive dogs. I looked at the crate, the fetus moved slowly. I don't remember if my son moved like that inside my belly. I noticed that its eye stayed open for a long time. I rubbed my hands along the jar, slid them down from the lid to the base and it seemed that the fetus was responding to my encouragement. Who gave birth to this thing that was capable of surviving inside a canning jar¿ I couldn't resist the impulse,

I stuck my pointer finger in, I wanted to see what would happen. At first, nothing, I only felt the placenta encompass my finger, then it lifted its neck until my finger reached its mouth, opened that little orifice, and before it was even all the way open it was sucking my finger so naturally it was like it was one of my own extremities. I felt a strange sensation, a type of affection I'd never felt before, like the affection we feel for pets. I quicky removed my finger, all affection was painful, the orifice continued simulating suction, the ghost of my finger still in its mouth. And even though it might seem incredible, I still felt the ghost of that sucking orifice squeezing around my finger. I realized then that I'd have company again, and it terrified me. Suddenly, the image of my grandmother was lodged in my brain. No question it was her who taught me about love and also about the horrible things love entails. She was always close to the pan. Night and day she stirred her gloop, if she didn't it would stick to the bottom. She'd look at me with those dark circles and grunt, don't be scared, girl, this is dead animal fat, I killed it myself 'cause I can't stand to see a beast suffer. You should learn to do the same, no point in thinking it's more righteous to watch the slaughter looking sad. More often than not the hand that deals the blow is the most merciful. Come here, give it a stir so you can see, the tallow isn't that thick, and later it makes a nice soap. I'd lean over the pan and feel that fetid and bubbling fat, and start to wonder how something so nasty could make fluffy white suds. In those moments I knew I wasn't made of anything nearly so diverse. I also stank, I also came apart in hot and sticky sweat. I was also a dying beast, but there was never a merciful hand to end it for me. I was an infected suture in God's face, because my roots ran deep and I wouldn't come out, I lived between the sewage and the water table, my pit was dug the instant I was born. My bones weigh more than my conscience and killing, to me, has always been easier than dying. *There's a crazy demented white simian sleeping between your vertebrae*. Hate might win out, but my vertebrae are dust—spinal osteoarthritis—the cartilage wore out and can't withstand the torture's weight. My mind returned to the present, I looked on top of the crate and the fetus was still there, contorting in the glass, the crate wobbled and the jar tipped to the side. I reached out and placed it in the middle again. Everything back in its right place, the beast clung to the sides of the jar and grunted like a pig. I asked myself why, when I bent down and opened that package, I hadn't thrown it to the dogs. Why'd I give this abominable thing the chance to live¿ I didn't have an answer. Despite those reflections, I breathed a sigh of relief, I was back in my room, everything still eyed me convulsively, and the ghosts were dead, at least for now. I stopped looking at the orphaned animal, I opened the door and went out into the garden, beneath the white fig, they were flowering for the first time; I thought I'd begin my rest, my head hurt and my body wasn't as lively as it used to be, everything required more effort than normal. But it wasn't long before one of those strange little men arrived to tell me the Poet was dead. It was incredible how he managed to give the worst news possible without furrowing his brow, without crying or pretending to. I looked right in his black, beady eyes, and for a minute I thought he might be wrong. It would be better if he was wrong. The Poet was one of the few men who still managed to make my pussy wet. I felt the Poet's tongue circling my breasts, nibbling them with his little teeth, then with all my strength I removed his fingers from my underwear, but I let him put his dick in instead. The little man stood paralyzed in front of me, I rested my eyes on his pelvis and noticed he was hard, it was like he was reading my mind. I asked what happened, who'd killed him, he didn't respond, they still hadn't dropped the silent bit, even though they had already learned our dialect. A wasp circled my bellybutton, it was the first time I noticed I'd been born with one, I remembered the orphan in the glass again and started wondering if it had a bellybutton, then decided it lacked such an insignificant orifice. A horrible stomachache plagued me, it was like a white hole had just opened up in my insides. Even though the news had shaken me, I wasn't surprised, I knew he'd end up that way. I'd warned him there aren't many choices for a hallucinated man, writing is just an idiotic attempt at giving life to marionettes, but creation can't suppress representation. And representation only trivializes reality. I decided to get out of there and see the body with my own eyes, I knew where he used to sit and write. It took me a little while to get up, my legs weren't what they used to be, they couldn't handle much, the body rots long before the soul. Afraid I wouldn't show up in time to bury him, I ended up taking that strange little man with me so he could help with the body, even though for a long time now the Poet had only been skin and bones. When we arrived, I could see his skinny body stretched out next to the book, there weren't any signs of fracture, no bruises or signs of aggression of any kind, and, incredible as it may sound, he smelled worse than he did when he was living. He'd achieved what he craved so much, to write the first book of a new Era, there it was, over one thousand pages, the book that had cost him his life. It would definitely take more work to move the book than the body. By the size of it I guessed it was an epic, he must have written down all our small village's actions in perfect detail. I felt a certain nostalgia at seeing that book splayed out next to the corpse, both of them looking dead. He'd been so meticulous. The cover was beautiful, leather, my eyes were a little blurry but once I focused my vision I could make out the title—it was OM. I didn't understand what he was referring to, but I also didn't give it much thought, surely the name would be explained by the text. I crouched down beside the wax doll and tried to lift the book, but I couldn't, so I asked the strange little man for help, who didn't say a word and, his expression unmoving, lifted the book with incredible ease, like it didn't weigh more than a couple grams. I pulled the Poet into my lap, even though I was very weak I barely had to try, he weighed about the same as an empty box. It didn't take us long to cross the road and arrive in my yard again. I leaned the Poet up against the white fig, motioned with my head to the strange little man and he placed the book beside the corpse. Then I thanked him and said he could go, everything was all right, if he wanted he could invite his peers to the wake. I don't know what got into me, I thought the Poet might have liked having a cult around his body. I'd gather the flowers and cover him with them myself. The strange little man nodded. There, alone, I figured was the right time to read the book. Even though I don't see anything good about writing, I was curious; I thought, who knows, maybe I'd be in there; after all, I'd been an important person in that town, I'd been an important person for the Poet. I started to leaf through the tome, the Poet began with an epigraph: "The word is a grunt when compared with the silence of God." I continued flipping through all one thousand five-hundred pages and I couldn't believe what I was reading, it was unreal! After reading from the first page to the last, I decided to go backwards, I started from the last page and read through to the table of contents. There had to be something wrong. I started to think I'd gone insane, then I suspected my eyes had finally worn out after all those years. I went inside the house and went through all the cupboards until I found a jar with a thick base, I grabbed a rock and broke the jar, then kept just the bottom, I could use it as a magnifying glass. I went back to the garden and crouched down next to the book. I leafed through it again, now with the help of the lens, page by page, patiently. My vision was clear now and I also wasn't crazy, on every page in letters like scribbles:

-OMMMMMMMMMM–OMMMMMMMMMMMMM-

-OMMMMMMMMMMM-OMMMMMMMMMM-

-OMMMMMM-OMMMMMMMMMMMMMMM-

- O M M M M M M M M M M M M M -

- O M M M M M M M M M M M M M -

- O M M M M M M M M M M M M M M -

- O M M M M M M M M M M M M M M M M M -
-O M M M M M M M M M M-O M M M M M M M M M M M M-
- O M M M M M M M M M M M M M M M M -
- O M M M M M M M M M M M M M -
- O M M M M M M M M M M M M M M M -
- O M M M M M M M M M M M M M M M -
-O M M M M M M M M M M M-O M M M M M M M M M M M M M-
- O M M M M M M M M M M M M M -
- O M M M M M M M M M M M M M M M -
- O M M M M M M M M M M M M M M M M M -
- O M M M M M M M M M M -
- O M M M M M M M M M M M M M M -
O M M M M M M M M M M M M -
M O M M M M M M M M M M M M M M M -
- O M M M M M M M M M M M M M M -
- O M M M M M M M M M M M -
- O M M M M M M M M M M M M M M M M M M M M -
-OMMMMMMMMMM OMMMMMMMMMMMMMM-
- O M M M M M M M M M M M M M M M M -
- O M M M M M M M M M M M -
- O M M M M M M M M M M M M M M M -
- O M M M M M M M M M M M M -
- O M M M M M M M M M M M M M M -
-O M M M M M M M M M M M M-O M M M M M M M M M M-
- M M M M M M M O M M M M M M M M M M M M -
-OMMMMMMMMMM OMMMMMMMMMMMMMM-
- M M M M M M M M M M O M M M M M M M M M -

- O M M M M M M M M M M M M M -
- M M M M M M M M M M M M M M M M M -
- O M M M M M M M M M M M M -
- O M M M M M M M M M M M M M M M M M M M M M M M -
-OMMMMMMMMM OMMMMMMMM. A horrible sensation gnawed at the soles of my feet, I opened the door to my house, I needed some water, my sight was blanching the entire garden. I only felt worse after, since upon entering I saw the philosopher from behind, he was standing in front of the crate, his eyes locked on the fetus, he was about to plunge his finger inside the jar but when he noticed I was there he recoiled and the shadow of his arm came apart in the air. What happened¿ You're white, you look like you've just seen a ghost. What are you doing here. I thought you were off in other lands. Yeah, I know, I wasn't brave enough to show up earlier, you'll have to forgive me... What do you want from me¿ Did you come to see with your own two eyes that I'm old, that I'm not the same as I used to be¿ No, no, my dear, I'm not that cruel, don't take it that way... I just wanted to remember old times... Don't lie to me, you aren't here for that, you wouldn't even be able to fuck these days, you're old too. Tell me what you really want. You're right, I'm also old, and yes, it's true, I need you. I don't know if you're up to date on what's been happening in the village. How could I not be¿ A whore knows everything. Well, I've been appointed as judge. You're joking! You, a judge¿ Philosophers make terrible scales. Don't say that, and anyways, it's been a long time since I was a philosopher... I don't think I ever was, really. What do you

mean you weren't, what about all those ideas¿ I was just young and dumb. You're scaring me! How could someone who spoke so much about transparency accept a role like that, you know well there aren't judges in this land, there's just an executioner, you won't be the judge, you'll be the executioner! I'm sorry, my love, but I didn't choose it, I was named, well… I was the only one who could take it on. Sure, and what do you want with me¿ To ask for my approval¿ You can have it, make as many heads roll as you want, there aren't that many around here anyways. It's not that, I wanted to ask you about your son. You armchair philosopher, you must be joking! What could you possibly want with my son¿ It's too early to say, I can't tell you anything right now, but I'd like you to tell me where he is. And if I refuse¿ What will you do¿ Will you send me to the guillotine¿ Don't joke about that, I would never and you know it. No, I don't. I just need to talk to him, gather some information. That's a mouth it's hard to pry words from, unlike you, he was never prone to chit-chat. I can try. It won't be worth it. My dear, you have to understand, ever since these strange little men showed up around here, horrible crimes have been happening, we can't let it go on unchecked, if we don't do anything it will all end up like before. My dear friend, I wish things were the way they were before, you're treating me like you don't even know me. I'm sorry, I don't have anything against those strange men, and we don't even know if it's their fault. Everything points to it. Funny, when you were a philosopher you used to care about evidence. And that's what I'm doing. Speaking of evidence, what is a jar with a fetus inside doing in your home¿ What animal is that¿ That's a long story, I'll tell you some other time. All right, I'll see myself out, when your son comes back tell him I need to talk to him, and Flamenca as well. Did you notice anything strange about them, did you notice red marks all over their bodies¿ I didn't see anything, they rarely come through here and never give me time to inspect them, you're looking for a bee in a marimbondo nest. And if you don't mind, I would be grateful if you let me bury my dead. Forget it, my dear, let me kiss your forehead. He took my head in his shaky hands and extended his withered lips to my large forehead. And I thought, there's no elegance in old age. He left, one of the few men I've watched leave without touching my vagina, without sticking his hands in to make sure no honey comes out. The first thing I had to do was find an urn, a wooden box, I thought of taking the one from the living room, but I remembered the fetus was on top of the crate and I didn't think it was appropriate to move it from its customary location. I decided to go to the little men's house. When I arrived, they opened the door mechanically, placed themselves one beside the other, and all of them had erections. Even though age had dried me out on the inside, that image made me plump right up. They turned me around and one by one went in and out quickly until a single white stream fertilized the floor. I got up and said I was looking for a coffin for the Poet. They immediately went to the other room and brought back a big heavy box. Because I had a hard time carrying it, one of them got himself ready to help me take it home. There was a crowd in the distance, all the men I'd slept with were holding vigil over the dead. I saw the bookie's white suit, the machinist's large and erect member, I saw the little feet of the others I'd slept with whose names I don't remember, I heard the philosopher's metaphysical musings, I smelled Flamenca's rue smell and remembered our first orgasm. In one way or another, they were all there and the corpse seemed to smile, he, who spent his whole life seeking the solitude of holes had finally found it in those mute and distant faces. I passed through that mass of people with the little man in front of me, he opened the door with his feet, asked with a motion of his head where he should leave the box, and I told him to place it in the middle of the room so the corpse and the fetus could look at each other. I nodded thank you, said he could leave, that everything was fine. It would be good if you and yours came to the wake, I'll have everything ready by the time night opens its craw. He nodded. From the door, I watched him on the road, followed him as he passed through that mass of men and disappeared. I went inside and washed my hands again. I went to the fig and grabbed the Poet's body, it seemed even lighter now than it did before. I laid him out in the latrine and went back to the garden to grab a handful of rue. I put a little water on to boil, then put the sticks and rue leaves inside. A nice smell spread through the house and again, I felt Flamenca's presence. I mixed a little cold water in a bowl and threw the infusion in. I grabbed a scrap of fabric and started bathing the body, I found it strange, the Poet had stopped shedding those smelly scales after he died, his skin was now smooth and uniform like a newborn baby's. His pants were dirty and torn, I unbuttoned and removed them, then I noticed that his dick was still as hard as ever; I started to clean him very carefully, massaging him a little, moving the rag across his chest and down to his groin, when I noticed that I was already riding the corpse and couldn't get down until I touched my clit and waited to climax. Soon I got off the cold cadaver and continued cleaning it. I went to my son's old trunk and found the Poet some clothes, my son didn't own many, so there wasn't much to choose from. I went back to the coffin and clothed the body, then I walked the road in search of branches and flowers, I didn't find much, but enough for a decent wake. I was almost ready now, I just needed a beverage to drink with the dead, I remembered that Flamenca had brought me a little barley water on one of her visits. Then all I had to do was wait for night to come, I grabbed a rock and sat down next to the Poet, facing the fetus, which leaned slowly to the left. I looked at its hands and they opened and closed until one of them moved to its mouth and the thing started sucking desperately. As soon as the shadows cast onto the corpse, the little men began arriving, all of them came, they entered in silence and positioned themselves around the coffin. Little by little the men mourning on the street came closer, but only the philosopher had the courage to burst through the door and enter. My condolences, I hope that when I go, there's also someone there to see to the preparations. I didn't say anything, only nodded my head. He knew very well that the executioner does the burying but can't be buried. He went quiet and returned his eyes to the animal in the jar, I didn't reprimand him, though I knew he wasn't there for the deceased, he was interested in that life exploding explicitly. The door squealed again, but it wasn't a man standing there, it was a skinny and mangy dog, it came in and laid down beneath the coffin. I went to touch it with my hands but mid-gesture decided against it, and instead let it be. I served the drinks and we waited together for daybreak. I was very tired and must have fallen asleep on top of the body, my back hurt when I woke up. There wasn't anyone else in the room except the dog, who was still sleeping in the same spot. I heard a noise in the yard and went to see who it was. Gaguinho lowered his head in a quick greeting, his hair was longer and grayer, but otherwise he was the same. I was tired, I could've kept blazing trails through my anguish, but I realized it was useless, I couldn't change what was done. I couldn't bring Aninha back, I couldn't invent a discourse that wasn't of my mouth, my mouth had been mourning a dead tongue. They say that time is an outstretched line and we can walk it freely, but I discovered that's another lie, it's a wrinkled line, an infinite fold we can't walk on once it's been ironed out. No man regurgitates the past. I learned a lot from Antonio Conselheiro, but it wasn't enough to be happy. He didn't have an answer to the question I asked. I admire you, friend, you managed to bury your dead instead of mourning them your whole life. I stayed quiet and watched that enigmatic figure, and for a moment I felt immense pity, pity like I've never felt before. Before me stood a naive farmer, a poor man who believed that words would save him from solitude. He never understood that for Aninha, speech would have been an empty ornament, his words wouldn't have saved her from boredom, they weren't worth anything. He held out his hands to me, he'd brought me a pile of moldy strawberries. I thanked him halfheartedly. He went on with his story, said he'd kept following Antonio Conselheiro for years and years, but ended up discovering you can't rip out an old wound by force, people change change leave home 'cause they crave other lands other faces they crave foreign features but the hurt remains, encrusted, a skin ailment that never heals, we are in exile, but we can't exile the ailment from us. I decided to stop in a little settlement, I started planting strawberries, I wanted them to be as perfect as the ones on Aninha's towels. But it was just a stupid thought I had, only the strawberries on the towels don't mold, in the hand of a man they rot quick. I moved my chin toward my torso in a sign of agreement. Can I stay here with you¿ And just for a little while, I'll be gone before summer, the end will come before then. How could I refuse¿ Make yourself at home, it'll be the three of us. What do you mean, three¿ Me, you, and the beast in the jar. Beast in the jar¿ It's a long story, I'll tell you some other time, for now all you need to know is they tossed a fetus on the doorstep and it ended up surviving in a canning jar. And the dog¿ Yeah, seems like he wants to stay too. In a way, sharing my home again made me happy, I barely saw Gaguinho, he spent most of his time in the garden tending the fig tree, but knowing he was there was soothing. The body had been in the box for three days and the dog was still motionless beneath it. I was thinking of getting the Poet out of there and burying him, but I was interrupted by a hasty knock at the door. Before I could open the latch the doctor entered, out of breath and almost shouting. Hurry up, show me, let's go! Are you crazy¿ What are you talking about¿ The Poet's body, where is it¿ What do you want with his body¿ The judge didn't tell you¿ He's allowed me to perform autopsies on the village dead, and as you know there aren't many people around here, so when I heard about the Poet I came running. The Poet doesn't need an autopsy, he's fine the way he is. I know, but I'm testing a new mummification technique, he's already dead and afterwards he'll stay right here, I can do the procedure in your home and if you want you can keep him after. Why the fuck would I want to keep a dead body in here with me¿ I don't know, to preserve the memory. I'm asking as a courtesy, the truth is you don't have a choice, the judge has already decided. So do what you're going to do and don't bother me. Wait a minute, what's that on that crate¿ It doesn't matter. What do you mean it doesn't matter¿ Of course it matters! It's phenomenal! How did you manage that¿ Why didn't anyone tell me about this fetus¿ It's incredible it's survived! I have to study it! It could represent a considerable advance in my practice! Stop acting crazy, you never wanted to be a doctor! You're an unkind whore, I didn't want to be one when I was young, but I've been dedicating my life to medicine for a long time now. I don't care, your knowledge never did anything for me.

Leave the jar where it is, if I need your services one day, I'll call you. Don't get upset, for now I'll be satisfied with the Poet, he'll take me a few days, but I won't forget that fetus, I'll be back to see it. I'll need to spend a couple days in your house to mummify him, but then I'll leave you in peace. I'm not young anymore, I'm very tired. I was also tired, so exhausted my labia wanted to crawl up inside my uterus and disappear, I wanted to be annihilated-sublimated by my own body. Gaguinho came up behind me, silently, put his hands on my shoulders and whispered something incomprehensible. I thanked him. My entire life I've been pierced by man's harpoon, but none have been able to penetrate me, maybe the Poet and the philosopher got close, but in the end they were corrupted, they got hooked by other urgencies. And I went on like a fish choking on its own smile. Now I was confined with an almost asexual being, an entity who's only known the climax of a single woman. I'd like to name it Ana, can it be named Ana¿ Confinement was certainly doing something horrible to that man's brains. What the fuck are you talking about¿ That jar fetus, can we call it Ana¿ How do you know it's a woman¿ That thing might not even be people. I know it's a woman, I feel it. I spent hours staring into its eyes and there's no way they belong to a man, men are too ironclad to speak with their eyes... It's better to wait, at some point that fetus will mature and then we'll decide its destiny. On the third day the doctor finished his work, he called me over to see, he was excited, said no mummification had ever been so perfect. I went into the living room and looked at the hard and plasticky body, and started wondering where the doctor saw perfection, all I saw was a nocturnal cobra shaking its tail and spreading terror. I quickly left the room and asked him to take the Poet away, I didn't want to see it anymore. Yes, I'll call one of those little men to help with the coffin, but don't forget I'll be back as soon as the fetus is born. You don't need to call anyone, Gaguinho can help you. I watched the three of them walk through the garden, then towards the road, I felt a small stirring, but I held back my tears, if I started howling at that point my bones would break and I'd turn into a blown-up hollow lizard. I went to the trunk and grabbed a Cuban cigar, lit it, closed my eyes and took a long drag. Flamenca was nearby and her smell, the taste of her clitoris made me salivate thick, white sputum. I lied on the ground and there she was, nasty, sticking her hand in my underwear, let's go, Muchacha, open wide, sticking her tongue in the movable soil-axis of my mouth, nibbling at my tits and peering at my broad face laughing waiting for my soaking smile. I fell asleep right there and was only awoken by the sound of Gaguinho opening the latch, I was too weak to get up—I spent three days and three nights in the same position. On the fourth day, I got up, my son and Flamenca were nearby, I could hear the zooming of the fly that rotted her eye, I could hear the fly galloping on her face, rubbing its legs together, I could hear it buffing its shell its back on the sun. I could hear the fly vomiting-regurgitating its orbit in my ear. I took a shower, fixed my hair, touched my vagina to see if it was still moist, if I could still open my phalanges, nails and fingers. I was sure, they had come. It was a horrible sight, the last time I saw them they had red marks, but now they had huge pustules and their whole bodies were covered in them. Flamenca's face was unrecognizable, a herd of horses had torn up her face and breasts. I couldn't look at them, I motioned for them to come inside, but like on previous visits, they refused with a shake of their heads. I asked Flamenca what happened and she muttered between her teeth that there had been an outbreak of smallpox in one of the villages they'd passed through. I asked them to stay, said the judge was looking for them. There's no reason for us to stay here, we'll keep moving, we're nomads, remember¿ It doesn't matter what you are, you're sick, you can't keep going, you'll die out there. We'll die either way, at some point these wounds will get worse and no one will be able to do anything about them. Flamenca was right, the trigger had been pulled, I saw death's spurs, the demon's calloused hand, the devil's nuptials, his dog, his eyes, his sperm running down their gullets. The carnivorous mare peered at them. Before they could leave, the philosopher arrived with two men I'd never seen before. I've come at the right time. What do you want with them¿ Unfortunately I have to take them. You're crazy, where do you want to take them¿ Can't you see they don't have much time¿ Lots of people are dying because of these pustules, they've been accused of spreading smallpox. They must be sacrificed. What are you talking about¿ They're not mangy dogs, you can't do this, you're so crazy your whole brain's turned to mush! They'll be hung tomorrow at noon. No one can stop it, I like you a lot, you know that, I respect our shared history, but don't confuse things, I'm doing this for the good of the village. You don't know what you're saying, I don't argue with crazy people. It was as if the noose was around my neck and my hands were bound. I couldn't do anything, I would have to watch the spectacle in silence, I would have to learn to pluck the larvae from my affection and move on, I would have to eat my uterus's rotten fruit. Nightmare, the mares of midnight galloped their muddy hooves over the ground. We have to face the mirror and not be fooled by the figure-fissure it sends in return. The eye is blind, stillborn, a piece of rotted flesh. I've walked and observed the scission of the femur and patella, I disdain all desire that ends in dust. They killed the white whale. I sleep beached in its groin. Hate's affection-carcass. They tied their hands behind their backs and led them away; they didn't resist, they let themselves be taken and they weren't afraid. I was already awaiting the execution well before dawn. A little before noon those strange little men placed themselves silently by my side, and in each face I saw a whore fucking her executioner. Then the two convicts were positioned near the noose. The philosopher feigned blindfolded eyes, but I saw the disgrace and all the shit hidden behind his false unseeing. My son would be the first to be executed. Only after the knot was tied and the suffocated throat sought relief and didn't find it, only after seeing the body still and the breath suspended did I yell at the philosopher. That child didn't just come from my bountiful womb, half of him was made of your contaminated sperm, your uncured gonorrhea. The philosopher let out an inaudible hiccup. Of them all, that was my worst revenge. I walked to Flamenca and whispered in her ear: you could have avoided all this, but you were a fool and curious and wanted to know the tempest of men. I couldn't see the expression on her face because her eyes had already been eaten by the white fly, I also couldn't see the lines on her face because the pustules were enormous and had deformed her completely. But I smiled, because I knew I'd managed to cast the blame on her. The sun was blanching the entire village, I looked up, worms gnawed at the sky. I went home, noticed the latch had rusted and fell into convulsive sobs. Gaguinho sat beside me and finally understood that the tongue is a dead organ moldy muscle. He stayed quiet. I spent the afternoon, the night, and the early morning removing serpents from my esophagus. I woke up, outside the body of the big white whale rotted. At the morning's end, I felt my breasts inflating and leaking milk, I looked at my feet and they were enormous. I started to feel pangs in my stomach and soon realized they were contractions, I rolled around in pain on the floor. The coffin wouldn't stop shaking, the fetus squirmed desperately and tried to bust through the jar. I cried out, the pangs worsened, I asked Gaguinho to get the doctor quick. He left, and half an hour later the doctor was there. He said he didn't really know how to help me, he'd never seen anything like that, but he'd try. As soon as he stopped his nervous chatter, my water broke. I felt my vagina soaking and dilated. The fetus kept trying to escape from the jar.

Okay, I'm going to try to take the baby out of the container, maybe the pain will stop when it's born. I nodded, I didn't have any better ideas. The mangy dog observed, attentive and nervous. The philosopher arrived and held my hand. You still remember the things I told you when we were young¿ It's all true, I still believe it all. It's the wheel of misfortune, you'll see! After all other incarnations, man will become woman and pay for all sins, he'll slough off in the mouth of the monster, that's what the other thinker said. But I take it further, I say more, I say man will be transformed into a whore's vagina. Man will be just a hollow space between a whore's legs. And then, he will free himself of his sins and come inside the monster's jaw. (S)he busted out of the jar, slid around on top of the crate. And it wasn't possible to see the genitals or decipher the sex. Was it male or female¿ I don't know, all we knew was we needed a woman. That's when the doctor intervened, he removed a rib from the mangy dog, opened h(is)er back, implanted the new rib, grafted some buttocks flesh to avoid a viscous scar, and stitched it up. Ana's revenge, beautiful and hateful. As I took her in my arms, I glimpsed my face in the orange frame and the epiphany came, this man who walled me in, flagellated me, tortured me, forced me to view the world squatting inside a prison, this man who threatened to tear up my pussy, rip out my clit, this man who confused me with a simian, a neanderthal, who forced me to gaze in a spherical mirror with no frame. This man who bound my feet while I masturbated. This white man-animal-monster who swallowed me and spit me out.

This man who inseminated me shoved an embryo in my guts. This demented man who contaminated me with syphilis. This executioner-man who flayed my skin hungrily, who tore out the nails of my pinkie toes. Who stuck his dick in me unceremoniously. This man who gnawed-chipped my bones. This man was me. This man was the grimace I hid behind my well-painted mask.

Márcia Barbieri has authored five novels and three short story collections. Her first novel, *Mosaico de Rancores*, was published in German in 2016 by Clandestino Publikationen, and she has been a finalist or semifinalist for many of Brazil's largest literary awards, including the São Paulo Prize for Literature in 2018 for *O Enterro do Lobo Branco*, and the Guarulhos Literature Award and the Oceanos Prize in 2019, both for *A Casa das Aranhas*.

Adrian Minckley is a Portuguese-to-English media and literary translator. Her work has appeared in or is forthcoming from *Your Impossible Voice, Two Lines, Firmament, Words Without Borders,* and *Calico*. Her first novel-length translation, João Reis's *The Devastation of Silence*, was published in 2022. She was awarded a 2021 PEN/Heim Translation Grant for her translation of *The Whore*.

SUBLUNARY EDITIONS is a small, independent press based out of Seattle, Washington, publishing in the field of contemporaneous literature, i.e. writing unbounded by era or geography. A selection of our titles can be found below. You can learn more about us at sublunaryeditions.com

FALSTAFF: APOTHEOSIS / Pierre Senges, tr. Jacob Siefring
926 YEARS / Kyle Coma-Thompson, Tristan Foster
CORPSES / Vik Shirley
A LUMINOUS HISTORY OF THE PALM / Jessica Sequeira
THE WRECK OF THE LARGE GLASS / PALEÓDROMO / Mónica Belevan
UNDER THE SIGN OF THE LABYRINTH / Christina Tudor-Sideri
UNDULA / Bruno Schulz, tr. Frank Garrett
STUDIES OF SILHOUETTES / Pierre Senges, tr. Jacob Siefring
FRAGMENTS FROM A FOUND NOTEBOOK / Mihail Sebastian, tr. Christina Tudor-Sideri
TWO STORIES / Osvaldo Lamborghini, tr. Jessica Sequeira
THE VOICES & OTHER POEMS / Rainer Maria Rilke, tr. Kristofor Minta
THE POSTHUMOUS WORKS OF THOMAS PILASTER / Éric Chevillard, tr. Chris Clarke
A CAGE FOR EVERY CHILD / S. D. Chrostowska
MORSEL MAY SLEEP / Ellen Dillon
HOMECOMING / Magda Isanos, tr. Christina Tudor-Sideri
RATIONALISM / Douglas Luman
ANECDOTES / Heinrich von Kleist, tr. Matthew Spencer
[TITLE] / [Name of author]
LETTERS FROM MOM / Julio Cortázar, tr. Magdalena Edwards
WHAT THE MUGWIG HAS TO SAY & SILVALANDIA / Julio Cortázar, Julio Silva, tr. Chris Clarke
RABELAIS'S DOUGHNUTS / Pierre Senges, tr. Jacob Siefring
THE LIGHTED BURROW / Max Blecher, tr. Christina Tudor-Sideri
TRANSPARENT BODY & OTHER POEMS / Max Blecher, tr. Christina Tudor-Sideri
SHAMMAI WEITZ / Isaac Bashevis Singer, tr. Daniel Kennedy
A FRIEND OF THE FAMILY / Yves Ravey, tr. Emma Ramadan & Tom Roberge
BEYOND / Horacio Quiroga, tr. Elisa Taber
DISEMBODIED / Christina Tudor-Sideri
CHIMERAS / Daniela Cascella
MYSTERY TRAIN / Can Xue, tr. Natascha Bruce
A PERFECTLY RUINED SOLITUDE / Kristofor Minta
WE THE PARASITES/ A. V. Marraccini
THREE DREAMS / Jean Paul & Laurence Sterne

VAGARIES MALICIEUX / Djuna Barnes
THE LAST DAYS OF IMMANUEL KANT / Thomas De Quincey
MARIA WUTZ / Jean Paul
IF YOU HAD THREE HUSBANDS / Gertrude Stein
FANTASTICKS / Nicholas Breton
IVAN MOSCOW / Boris Pilnyak
POEMS / Karl Kraus
NEWTON'S BRAIN / Jakub Arbes
A LOOKING GLASSE FOR THE COURT / Antonio de Guevara
A CYPRESSE GROVE / WIlliam Drummond of Hawthornden
MORNING STAR / Ada Negri
ZORRILLA, THE POET / José Zorrilla
POEMS / Miguel de Unamuno
ESSAYS, PARADOXES, SOLILOQUIES / Miguel de Unamuno
JOAN OF ARC / Jules Michelet and Thomas De Quincey
PAGES FROM THE DIARY OF A JACKASS / Ante Dukić
PREFACES / Jean Paul
THE CITY OF DREADFUL NIGHT AND OTHER WRITINGS / James Thomson
THE COLLECTED WORKS / Kathleen Tankersley Young
EXERCISES / Benajmín Jarnés
AT THE DOORS AND OTHER STORIES / Boris Pilnyak
SONNETS AND POEMS / Antero de Quental
GEBIR / Walter Savage Landor
HALLUCINATED CITY / Mário de Andrade
THE COLLECTED WORKS, VOLUME I / Emanuel Carnevali
THE COLLECTED WORKS, VOLUME II / Emanuel Carnevali
TWO STORIES / Jean Paul
BIOGRAPHICAL RECREATIONS FROM THE CRANIUM OF A GIANTESS **/** Jean Paul
THE COLLECTED POEMS / Amy Levy